SECRET OF THE
RED ARROW

HARDY BOYS
ADVENTURES™

#1 *SECRET OF THE RED ARROW*

FRANKLIN W. DIXON

ALADDIN   New York London Toronto Sydney New Delhi

ALADDIN

An imprint of Simon & Schuster Children's Publishing Division

1230 Avenue of the Americas, New York, NY 10020

First Aladdin paperback edition February 2013

Copyright © 2013 by Simon & Schuster, Inc.

All rights reserved, including the right of reproduction in whole or in part in any form.

ALADDIN is a trademark of Simon & Schuster, Inc.,

and related logo is a registered trademark of Simon & Schuster, Inc.

THE HARDY BOYS MYSTERY STORIES, HARDY BOYS ADVENTURES,

and related logo are trademarks of Simon & Schuster, Inc.

Also available in an Aladdin hardcover edition.

For information about special discounts for bulk purchases, please contact Simon & Schuster

Special Sales at 1-866-506-1949 or business@simonandschuster.com.

The Simon & Schuster Speakers Bureau can bring authors to your live event.

For more information or to book an event contact the Simon & Schuster Speakers Bureau

at 1-866-248-3049 or visit our website at www.simonspeakers.com.

The text of this book was set in Adobe Caslon Pro.

Manufactured in the United States of America 0113 OFF

2 4 6 8 10 9 7 5 3 1

Library of Congress Control Number 2012953643

ISBN 978-1-4424-6585-5 (hc)

ISBN 978-1-4424-4615-1 (pbk)

ISBN 978-1-4424-4619-9 (eBook)

CONTENTS

THE HOLDUP

1

FRANK

IT'S FUNNY TO THINK ABOUT HAVING ENEMIES.
Not funny ha-ha. Funny strange.

I was standing in line at the First Bayport Bank on Water Street. Dad had sent me here on an errand, explaining that the Hardy household believed in banking in person, not online. Mistakes were less common, he said, when the tellers had a face to remember. Even plain old Frank Hardy's face.

I knew it was just an excuse to get me out of the house. "You're spending too much time cooped up in front of a computer screen." Dad, Mom, Aunt Trudy, and my brother, Joe, each told me that at least five times a day.

Well, they weren't the ones who had to give a speech. That's right: In one week, yours truly had to get up in front of the entire Bayport High School student body to present my American history paper on civil liberties, which my teacher, Ms. Jones, had called "exceptional." I'd been really happy about that until I realized it would lead to mandatory public speaking. Thinking about it gave me turbocharged butterflies. I was embarrassed to admit it, but if there was one thing I truly hated, it was public speaking. D-day was right around the corner, and I didn't even have a final speech yet. I pretended to be "researching," but the reality was that I was turning into Joe: a world-class procrastinator.

The line in the bank was long, and the wait was boring. It had rained all morning, which meant drippy umbrellas inside. My sneakers were soaked through from the walk.

I took out my cell and texted Joe. We were going to meet up later at the Meet Locker to study. (That's a coffee shop, in case you were wondering. A popular hangout, it's open late, and they serve a mean Maximum Mocha.)

NO SIGNAL.

Typical, I thought. Bayport had become notorious for its spotty cell reception.

Staring down at my phone, I accidentally bumped into the person in front of me in line. "Sorry," I said. The guy glanced back. Then, eyes widening, he turned to face me.

It was Seth Diller, Bayport High's very own Quentin Tarantino.

"Oh. Hey, Seth," I said.

He studied me with his strange, unblinking, pale-blue eyes. He looked very highly charged for some reason, like he'd beaten me to the Meet Locker and drunk about twelve espressos. A few inches shorter than me, Seth was wearing a black turtleneck so tight it made me wonder if his brain was being deprived of oxygen. Finally he dipped a nod in my direction. "Frank," he said quietly.

I didn't know Seth very well. But he always had a camera in his hand. He was president of the Bayport High AV Club.

His specialty was monster videos. I'd seen a couple on the club website. Lots of fake tissue damage and gross-out effects. Joe appreciated that Seth took the time to make all his effects "in the camera"—meaning not digitally. No CGI for Seth. He was a purist. Joe was a fan, me not so much.

"Working on any new monster masterpieces?" I asked, just to be friendly.

He nodded. "Yes . . . in fact, I'm cooking up something really special."

"Really?"

He smiled. "That's right. I'm hoping this new movie will break my record of eleven thousand four hundred fifty-six views on YouTube."

I guessed that was impressive. "What's it about?" I asked.

He frowned and gave a shrug. "It's hard to describe."

I figured he didn't want to talk about it, so I just wished him luck and changed the subject. "Hey, how's your brother doing?" Tom Diller, Seth's older brother, had been badly wounded while serving with the marines in Afghanistan.

Seth grew quiet, and I was starting to feel sorry I'd brought up such a personal subject. That's when we heard the screams.

"Everybody stay where you are!" a voice yelled.

Three men with guns, each wearing a mask from a recent slasher movie, had entered the bank. They were moving fast, pistols in their outstretched hands. One disarmed the security guard, dropped the guard's gun in a trash can, and forced him to lie on the floor. Another locked the front doors. The third came toward us.

I'm not going to lie: I was shocked, and a little scared. I could feel my heart hammering in my chest like it was trying to break out. The truth is, I'd been in far stickier situations than this one, but you don't exactly expect to run into a bank robbery on a Saturday morning in a sleepy little town like Bayport.

Seth, standing right beside me, stiffened and made a panicky sound in his throat. Seeing his fear brought me back to my senses. "Stay calm," I whispered to him. "Do whatever they ask. Everything will be fine."

He was fumbling in his pocket. Glancing over, I saw him take out his smartphone. Hands shaking, he hurriedly tapped the screen until a wobbly image of his own feet came up. He had enabled the video cam.

He was going to record the robbery.

"Seth, listen to me very carefully," I said in an urgent whisper. "Do not do that. These men are wearing masks for a reason. Just put your phone away."

But he wasn't listening. He cupped his hand so the phone was partway concealed and held it low against his leg, angling out at the room, capturing the heist in action.

"Empty your pockets and your purses!" the third gunman yelled. He was my height and thin, wearing a bulky army jacket that didn't fit. "Nice and calm, people. No sudden moves. We don't want to hurt anybody."

The gunman who had locked the doors joined him. "But we will shoot anyone who gets in our way!" he shouted. He rushed to one of the tellers' windows and proceeded to collect money from behind the counter.

Army Jacket began taking valuables from the people standing in line. Rings, necklaces, and wallets disappeared into a canvas bag he was carrying. He made quick work of it. My mind was racing. What would be the reaction of the gunmen if they saw Seth recording them? It would depend on a million factors. How experienced they were. How nervous. How desperate. Were these men killers?

Army Jacket reached Seth, standing right by my side. I held my breath. The gunman paused only for an instant while Seth dropped his wallet and wristwatch into the canvas bag in one movement. He hadn't seen Seth's phone in his other hand. I breathed a two-second sigh of relief. Then Army Jacket was facing me.

Something strange happened then. Army Jacket just stood there, letting the moment drag on too long. He didn't say anything. He didn't take my watch or my wallet. He didn't even seem all that threatening. He was just . . . staring at me.

Did he know me? It was possible. Even though my brother

and I are supposed to be officially "retired," we'd put away a fair share of criminals in our time. Maybe this guy had been sent to prison, courtesy of Frank and Joe Hardy, and had just gotten his release.

See, our dad, Fenton Hardy, was once a world-famous detective. Growing up, Joe and I would help him on his cases. Then we began tackling mysteries on our own. We were proud of our successes. But after one too many close calls, things started to get a little out of hand, for reasons having to do with private investigators' licenses (we didn't have any), insurance (none of that, either), and the threat of being sued by every hoodlum we ever put under a citizen's arrest. Which is not how my brother and I wanted to spend the remainder of our teenage years, provided we're lucky enough to survive them. Some of us even have hopes of college one day . . . of a scholarship . . . of a normal life.

So with a few phone calls, including references from our principal and assurances to the police chief and state attorney general, we "retired." Officially, it stays that way—for all the Hardys. Our dad writes books on the history of law enforcement. And Joe and I go to high school.

That cozy arrangement, a.k.a. "the Deal," lasted about a month before Joe and I started going crazy. Maybe being a detective is something in your blood. I don't know.

Since then we've started taking the occasional case for a good cause or to help a friend, but we try to keep it confidential. And we deny everything. We don't consider it lying, just being prudent. We haven't told our dad, which makes me feel a bit guilty, but I get the feeling he suspects.

Not that it mattered right now. All that mattered was that Army Jacket's arm had slowly fallen to his side. His gun was pointed at the floor. Like he'd forgotten about it. Now was my chance.

I was about to grab the gun and wrestle it out of his hand, but his accomplice hollered, "Hey! What are you doing?"

Shocked back into the moment, Army Jacket raised his gun again. My chance was gone. I'd blown it. I could see the tiny mouth of the black barrel, aimed between my eyes. He was about to fire!

2

SEEING DOUBLE

JOE

I WAS STARING INTO A FACE I'D KNOWN MY ENTIRE life: my big brother Frank's. For a dizzy second or two, I forgot where I was and what I was doing.

It had totally slipped my mind that Frank had been sent on a phony errand down to the bank. Everybody in the Hardy family agreed he had been spending way too much time on the computer lately, and that he needed to go out and get some exercise and fresh air. The rain shower was just a bonus. Besides, Mom and Dad did all the household banking online. It is the twenty-first century, after all.

When I saw Frank, I almost blurted out his name. I caught myself just in time. But there had to be some way I could let him know it was me in the Michael Myers mask (the one from *Halloween*, you know). How could I signal to him? How could I let him know?

For a second, I thought about speaking to him in sign. Frank and I are both pretty fluent in American Sign Language. I could keep it simple: B-B G-U-N.

Letting him know, first of all, that I was just holding a BB gun. An unloaded one at that. It was the most important thing to communicate if we were going to stop these idiots!

But I'd better back up a little bit. You're probably wondering how Joe Hardy came to be holding up a bank in the company of two hardened criminals in the first place.

I had been on my way down to the Locker to meet Frank. (It's actually called the Meet Locker, which I think is kind of a stupid name. Most kids seem to agree and just call it the Locker.) Frank was all worked up about his speech, which was (as he had told me a million times) exactly one week away. Anyway, I was supposed to help him with it.

As I walked past the alley behind the bank, a big guy in a Michael Myers mask—just like the one I was wearing now—darted out from behind a car and yanked me off my feet. Now, before you call me a wuss, I do know judo (I'm a green belt). But the business end of a nine-millimeter Glock was pressed right up against my gut, so I played along.

It was not the first time I'd had a gun trained on me by some hoodlum. Frank and I had been solving crimes since we were little. We had to keep it on the down low nowadays, of course, because we kept getting sued. But the situation wasn't completely unfamiliar to me.

Mr. Glock dragged me over to a van. The door was wide open. Inside, a woman was squirming and whimpering, and when I took a closer look I recognized Mrs. Steigerwald, the owner of Bayport's bowling alley, Seaside Lanes. A big guy was holding another gun and had a hand clamped over her mouth, but he lifted it just long enough for her to shout, "Joe! Help m—"

She was wearing a baseball cap and these big, 1970s-style sunglasses—her usual getup—and she was so terrified, her glasses seemed to be fogging up. It was awful. The other gunman told me I had to help them rob the bank . . . or she'd "get it." Their partner hadn't shown up, he said, so they were a man short. Then the first guy tossed a big, greasy-looking army jacket at me and handed me another *Halloween* mask and the BB gun.

I racked my brain, but I couldn't see any way out. Poor Mrs. Steigerwald was about to hyperventilate.

"Don't worry, Mrs. S," I assured her, putting on the army jacket and the mask. "It'll all be over really quick. Then I'll come right out to check on you."

"All r-right . . . J-Joe," she answered through chattering teeth. Which surprised me, since she normally called everybody plain old "you." I didn't think she knew my name. I was always "You—the blond Hardy." But I let it slide, thinking she was just terrified.

Sixty seconds later, I was a felon.

Have you ever tried to hold up a bank with the sole aim of keeping anyone from being hurt? It's quite a high-wire act.

"Hey!" one of my accomplices barked at me now, snapping me back into the present. I'd been staring at Frank, trying to figure out how to communicate with him. "What are you doing?" he demanded.

There was no chance to team up with my brother at the moment. It was too risky. I just needed to get this ordeal over with as soon as possible. I took Frank's wallet and moved on.

The next customer in line brought me to a halt. This time I couldn't hide my shock.

"Um . . . Mrs. Steigerwald?" I said. My voice was muffled through the mask.

Mrs. Steigerwald looked freaked out—and mad. She wasn't wearing her hat and glasses now, and her bright-red hair stuck out at crazy angles. Her green eyes—a really memorable shade—stared at me suspiciously. She clutched her purse, getting ready to hit me with it. "What do you want, you?" she asked.

Now I was really confused. How was Mrs. Steigerwald standing right in front of me? If she was in the bank, who was out in the van being held captive? How could she be in two places at once?

"Were you just outside?" I asked her.

She looked confused. "When?"

"Like, two minutes ago."

"No," she replied. "I've been here for the past half hour, discussing Seaside Lanes's bank loan with Tom Baines." The color started returning to her cheeks as she got going. "Which I wouldn't need to do if the young people in this town would tear themselves away from their screens once in a while for some good, clean, healthy bowling!"

I took a deep breath, set my gun on the floor, and stepped away from it. Then I raised my hands over my head.

Frank nearly knocked the wind out of me when he tackled me and wrestled me to the ground. My brother looks skinny, but he has some power. I didn't resist. The bank erupted in chaos. People screamed. I caught a glimpse of the other two robbers ducking out the side door. The security guard ran over and put a knee in my back.

Frank ripped the mask off my face. To his credit, he didn't say anything. He just frowned.

"There's a really good explanation," I said.

"I bet there is," Frank answered.

Before I could get that explanation out, though, Bayport's finest were on the scene. Our town might have lousy cell phone reception, but I guess the landlines worked just fine.

I was in cuffs and out the door before I could say another word.

Frank offered some good parting advice: "Joe, don't say anything until Dad and I get to the station."

I nodded and gave him a behind-the-back thumbs-up.

The police cruiser was waiting at the curb. The officers put me in the back, slammed the door, and took off.

Now, I know Frank told me not to say anything, but I didn't see any harm in being friendly. I'm a people person. Besides, I was just relieved the whole ordeal was over without anyone getting hurt. I figured together, we would sort this whole thing out.

So I said, "I know it sounds funny, but I am so glad to see you guys."

They didn't answer. No problem. For the present, I was a robbery suspect, caught in the act. Not the kind of person most cops would want to be friendly with. I wasn't offended.

Then a thought occurred to me. "How did you guys get there so quick?" I asked. "Was there a silent alarm? Or were you just passing by?"

Unsurprisingly, they kept up the silent routine.

As we cruised down Orchard Street, my gaze shifted out the window to a familiar yellow scooter, parked in a driveway. I felt a little tingle in my chest. She was home. Janine Kornbluth, that is.

The police cruiser took the corner at Starboard and Main. We were a block from police department headquarters. I began preparing myself for booking and getting my mug shot taken. (Sadly, this was not the first time I had been inside a jail cell.) But instead we sped up.

"Hey," I said. "You missed the turn."

We passed the station, gathering speed. Main Street

leads straight out of town and becomes State Road 17. We passed the last houses. Then there was nothing but pine trees growing tall and straight all around us.

Was I being kidnapped? I stared hard at the police officers, then noticed a detail about the hefty one behind the wheel. He had a scar on the back of his left hand—kind of a pink crescent moon. One of the guys in the bank heist had had the same scar! I should've noticed it sooner.

These guys weren't the police—they were the bank robbers!

Now I realized what had happened: The gunmen must have been wearing these police uniforms under their jackets. They had rushed out of the bank, dumped their masks, jackets, and the loot, and then dashed right back in to "arrest" me. No wonder the cops had been so quick.

My ordeal wasn't over after all.

A sharp pain in my wrists made me wince. I made an effort to relax my arms. I'd been straining at my handcuffs. Crazy, I know, but I was just starting to realize how mad I was.

These hoods had hijacked my morning, scared a bunch of innocent people witless, robbed a bank using me as a dumb accomplice, and now were getting clean away. And who knew what they planned to do with me now? What if their cruel tricks weren't over?

At Satellite Road, five miles outside the Bayport city limits, the cruiser slowed to a stop. The gunmen got out, pulled me out, and uncuffed me. "Start walking," the hefty one said. He pointed back into town. "That way." They got back in and drove off in the opposite direction.

I followed them. Admittedly, not very fast. But I was jogging along well enough.

Ahead of me, the cruiser stopped. The reverse lights came on. They backed up until they were beside me again. The driver's-side window rolled down.

"What do you think you're doing, kid? We told you to walk the other way."

I stared back at them without answering. I didn't open my mouth. I didn't even blink. I was done cooperating with these clowns.

They looked at each other and shrugged. "He'll never keep up on foot," the skinny one said. "Not if you gun it."

The hefty one nodded and stomped on the accelerator. The cruiser spit gravel and shot away. Within ten seconds it was gone from my view.

I sighed, turned, and began the slow walk back into town. Oh well, at least it had stopped raining.

When I got home, dirty and tired, the real cops were waiting for me. Luckily, after I told my story I avoided the booking, the mug shot, the taking the laces out of my shoes. I was told I wouldn't be charged with anything, and they left.

After they were gone, waiting for me on the kitchen table was a treat from Aunt Trudy: some kind of delicious sauce on top of homemade, ribbony pasta. I didn't know what it all was, but it was terrific.

Aunt Trudy lived in a little apartment above the garage. We called our aunt Green Thumb Trudy because she was crazy for gardening. She went to meetings on the subject of gardening and belonged to several gardening societies in the area. She also had a wicked sense of humor. My late lunch had come with a note attached: *For the Jailbird*.

Frank sat with me and gave me the final pieces of the puzzle while I ate.

After all I'd been through, here's the kicker: It all turned out to have been some sort of prank!

Mrs. Steigerwald was never under any threat. The woman I saw in the van must have been a double who'd gotten hold of a similar baseball cap and sunglasses. She may have even been wearing a bright-red wig. I'd been completely fooled.

All the loot from the holdup was found in the alley next to the bank in a cake box with a note that said, *Just kidding! LOL!* The police would return all the personal items and cash once they'd had a chance to dust for fingerprints.

Frank watched me as I finished up my lunch special and rinsed my plate. "Are you okay?" he asked after a moment. "You must have had a crazy day. I was worried about you."

Sometimes it's nice to have a brother.

CONSEQUENCES 3

FRANK

FTER THE FIFTH SIGH, I PUT THE photos down. "Okay, what's wrong?"

Joe had been looking through the Frank Hardy Known Criminal Index, a collection of mug shots and wanted posters I kept in my briefcase. But his eyes had glazed over, and his leg was bouncing in place.

"Did you ever stop and ask yourself *why*, Frank?"

"Why what?"

"Why people do the things they do . . . Why the Earth revolves around the Sun . . . Why we get involved in every kind of crazy trouble that crops up around here . . ."

I couldn't hear the rest of his answer. The decibel level in the Bayport High cafeteria was, as ever during lunch period, at the hollering point.

Joe toyed with his meal for a bit. He'd ordered his usual: the special of the day. I don't think he actually prefers one dish over another. He just likes variety.

I knew something was bugging him. After the cops left Saturday, he'd been in typically high spirits. But later, his mood had shifted, and he'd barely spoken two words since.

My blond-haired, blue-eyed brother is an unlikely one to sulk. In fact, he's one of the sunniest people I knew. But every once in a while something would get under his skin. He wouldn't bring it up right away. First he'd talk about something else. Finally he'd work his way around to what was really going on in his head. I knew I didn't have long to wait.

I was right.

He had been staring at a stack of photos of various white males between the ages of twenty and forty, but I could tell he wasn't really seeing their faces. (We'd been hoping he would be able to identify the phony cops who had briefly kidnapped him after the bank holdup on Saturday, but so far no luck.) All at once, he looked at me in alarm and said, "Am I a major-league sucker or something? Sort of Mr. Gullibility?"

"No."

"Do I have a sucker's face?"

I wanted to laugh. But I didn't. "A sucker's face? No. Why?"

"Well, look what happened: First I got taken in by a bunch of phony bank robbers. Then I got tricked by someone pretending to be Mrs. Steigerwald. And then I let myself get busted by fake cops!"

So that was it.

I was about to tell him I didn't think he was any more gullible than I was, whatever that was worth, but a voice interrupted our conversation:

"Dude, that was sick!"

Laughter echoed from the table next to ours. I looked up and saw a bunch of football players staring down into somebody's smartphone screen. As I looked, one of the players—Neal "Neanderthal" Bunyan—glanced up and met my eye.

Uh-oh. Neanderthal, Joe, and I were not exactly friends.

"Yo, Frank!" he yelled now, grabbing his friend's phone and holding it up so I could see it. "You seen this? It's your big movie debut!"

Big movie debut? I looked at Joe, who seemed to share my sense of wariness. Last I'd checked, I didn't have a feature film in production.

"What do you mean, Neander—er—Neal?" Joe asked.

Neanderthal got up from his table and walked over, still holding the smartphone. "Someone just messaged this link to my buddies," he said, holding it up so we could see the screen. It was a YouTube clip. He hit play, and Joe and I frowned at each other and watched.

The second the picture came up, my mouth dropped

open. It was me—at the bank yesterday. First I was shot from behind, standing in line, minding my own business. Then the screen moved to capture the "robbers" entering the bank, brandishing their "guns." Everyone screamed, and the bank robbers yelled at us to stay calm, then that they'd shoot anyone who didn't cooperate.

After a few more seconds, the screen dissolved to black, and then words flashed up in bright-red capital letters:

WHAT WOULD YOU DO?

And then:

PANIC PROJECT!
COMING THIS SUMMER!

I frowned again and looked up at Joe. He looked just as puzzled as I felt. "What was that?"

"That," I replied, handing the phone back to Neanderthal, "is what I think is supposed to become a viral video."

Neanderthal was laughing. "So, let me bet on what happens next," he said, turning around to make sure his buddies were watching. "Frank, I'm going out on a limb to say you pee your pants. Sorry, maybe I should have said 'spoiler alert.'"

I avoided Neanderthal's eyes as I wiped my mouth, tossed my napkin on my tray, and stood up. "Let's go, Joe."

"Awww, don't be embarrassed," Neanderthal chided,

chuckling. "I'm sure I would have been real scared if the same thing had happened to me. I mean, not as scared as you look, but scared."

Joe was still working on his special of the day. "Really?" he asked. "We're done with lunch?"

I nodded. "Really."

Joe looked disappointed, but he grabbed his tray and followed me away from our table. "What's up?"

I was looking around the cafeteria. "We need to find Seth Diller."

Joe looked around too. "Why?"

"Because he took that video."

I wasn't seeing Seth anywhere around the cafeteria. Then I remembered that some of the AV Club kids ate in the AV room. And Seth, as you might imagine, was big into the AV Club. Like president-three-years-running big.

Joe looked confused. "Wait, he shot that?" he asked. "Seriously? How would he have known to do that?"

I shook my head. "Not sure. He shot it with the video camera in his phone."

Joe furrowed his brows. "But . . . that makes it seem like Seth was involved. . . ."

"And he staged it all," I finished. "Like one of his stupid monster videos. Come on." I grabbed Joe's arm and led him up the back staircase toward the AV room. I don't usually have much of a temper—I'm a thinker, not a fighter—but I have to admit, the closer I got to Seth Diller, the more I wanted to punch him in the face. Had he really staged an entire bank robbery for the sake of some dumb movie project? Hadn't he ever heard of actors? Hadn't he ever heard of scripts?

Sometimes I think reality television is ruining our culture.

"Hey," I said, plowing through the door to the AV room. Seth sat with his AV cronies on a set of stairs near the back, surrounded by a maze of DVD players and old-school televisions on carts.

He looked surprised to see us. "Hey, Frank," he said, looking a little nervous. I understood his wariness. I mean, Seth and I had probably exchanged five words, total, in the entire year before the bank robbery. Now I was hunting him down on his "turf."

"My brother and I need to talk to you," I said. "Privately."

After a few seconds, Seth nodded. "Ah—okay."

He got up and walked over to us, and I held the door open for him to pass through. Then I walked over to a quiet corner of the hallway, by a window, and gestured for Seth to follow.

"What's this about?" he asked quickly, looking uncomfortable.

"It's about the video you shot on Saturday," I replied, crossing my arms. "Of the robbery. Remember?"

Seth looked at me blankly. I don't think the expression in his pale-blue eyes changed at all. "What do you mean?"

I sighed. So we were going to do it this way. "I'm talking about the video you took on your phone," I said, and then paused to wait for the recognition to spark in his eyes. But none came. "Come on, Seth. I saw it."

Seth gulped. It was nearly unnoticeable but for the lump traveling down his throat. "I didn't shoot anything. Is that all? Because we were kind of in the middle . . ."

Joe gestured at Seth's pocket, where the outline of his smartphone was clearly visible. "Then you won't mind if I borrow it for a sec?" he asked.

Seth frowned. "What?"

"Your phone." Joe gestured at Seth's pocket again. The top of the phone was peeking out. "I have just remembered that I need to call our aunt Trudy and remind her to buy some zucchini for dinner tonight, because I'm having a craving. Okay?"

Seth looked unsure how to react. Yes, this was a ridiculous request, but his phone was in plain sight. He was caught. "I really don't have time. . . ."

"It'll only take a second." Joe held out his hand.

Seth looked from Joe to me and back again. He didn't lose his composure, but very deliberately reached into his pocket and pulled out the phone. He looked at the screen for just a moment before Joe pulled it out of his grasp.

Joe moved closer to me and held out the phone so I could see it. The background was a particularly gory scene from one of Seth's most popular flicks. Joe didn't even bother pretending to make a call. He went straight to the "Videos" folder and clicked on it. A list popped up:

Roadkill cat.mov

Cool sunset.mov

Bankheistraw.mov

"That's it," I said, pointing.

Joe clicked on the video, and after a few seconds of buffering, it came up. The same video of me at the bank that Neanderthal had shown us just moments before.

Seth swallowed again, then looked down at the floor.

"Check his sent e-mails," I suggested on a whim. Joe pulled them up, then chuckled.

"There it is," he said, showing me the screen again. Sure enough, it was the same e-mail containing the link to the Panic Project trailer.

I looked up at Seth, whose eyes looked slightly buggier than usual. Other than that, he gave no outward indication of fear.

"Maybe we should go somewhere more comfortable," I suggested. "I think you have a lot of explaining to do."

HARMLESS 4

JOE

WHAT I DON'T UNDERSTAND," PRINCIPAL Gorse was saying as he crossed his good leg over his bad one, "is why you couldn't tell people what was going on. We've all seen movies, Seth. They have actors, scripts. If you know the ship on-screen isn't really sinking, does that make *Titanic* any less sad?"

Seth took in a quick breath. He looked like he was struggling to keep his composure. "Principal Gorse, I mean . . . come on."

The principal looked to the rest of us—me, Frank, and Officer Olaf, who had been sent in when the Bayport PD heard that we'd learned something about the bank robbery—for support.

"I think what he's trying to say," I jumped in, "is that real emotions are always more interesting to watch than fake ones. That's part of the appeal—that there is no script. Anything could happen."

Seth looked at me and smiled. "Exactly. I was performing a cinematic experiment. How would people react when they were put in these crazy, seemingly dangerous situations? What would happen?"

"And what happened in this case," Officer Olaf said, moving from his spot leaning against the front of Principal Gorse's desk, "was awfully lucky for you, Seth. Nobody got hurt. Nobody panicked and had a heart attack." He paused, standing right in front of Seth and looking down at him with serious brown eyes, running his fingers over his droopy mustache. "But you realize that was just luck, don't you?"

Seth looked up at Officer Olaf, defiant. I could tell he wasn't going to back down. "I didn't hurt anybody, Officer Olaf. It was never my intention to hurt anybody. It was just a harmless prank."

Frank, who was sitting next to me on a bench against the wall, huffed. "But you did kind of rob a bank," he pointed out.

Seth glared at him, surprised. "I did not," he insisted. "I staged a bank robbery, but we gave everything back."

"But in that moment," Frank said, getting to his feet, "I, and everybody else in that bank, really believed we might die. Make the wrong move, and you could have shot us full of holes. I'm sure lots of people were wondering whether they would make it out of the bank alive."

Seth frowned. He looked down at the floor for a second, then back into Frank's eyes. "I told them afterward that it was just a joke."

"But what if something had gone wrong?" Principal Gorse asked. He leaned across his desk. "Seth, you don't seem to get it here. Bank robberies are serious business. People panic. They act violently if they think it will save their lives. They feel terror that doesn't go away just because you leave a note saying it was only a joke."

Seth shifted uncomfortably, but his expression didn't change. "I take risks for my art," he said simply.

Officer Olaf sighed and turned to Principal Gorse. "Do you want to tell him what his punishment from you is? Because I'm about ready to take this kid down to the station house and straighten him out there."

Seth frowned again. Now he was looking a little nervous. "I'm being charged with a crime?" he asked.

Principal Gorse took a deep breath and said, "Seth, I'm afraid I have no choice but to suspend you for three days for cyberbullying your fellow students."

Seth jumped to his feet. "Cyberbullying?" he cried. "What?"

Principal Gorse gestured to Frank and me. "These two gentlemen were in your video."

Seth glared at me. "But they weren't even—"

"I'm afraid it's school policy."

Seth bit his lip, still glaring. He looked from me to Frank to Principal Gorse. "This is—"

But Officer Olaf didn't let him finish. "Now you have to come with me, Seth," he said, standing up. "You have the right to remain silent. Anything you say . . ."

Officer Olaf continued to read Seth his Miranda rights as Seth looked from him to Principal Gorse, stammering. "But—but—I didn't—"

"Criminal mischief," Officer Olaf said, moving close enough to Seth to wave a pair of handcuffs in his face. "You created a major disruption this weekend, Seth—diverting the police force and panicking citizens. I get that you didn't really rob a bank. But it turns out, pretending to rob a bank is pretty bad too." He jingled the cuffs again. "I'd rather not use these. Think you can walk out with me like a big boy— no trouble?"

Seth was still glaring at Officer Olaf, but his lower lip was starting to wobble. He took one last look around the room, and when he spotted me, his face flushed with anger. "Darn it, Joe! I thought you liked my videos! I thought you were cool!"

I sighed. I mean, I did feel bad for the kid. In his warped way, he was pretty talented. "Listen, Seth, if putting me in cuffs and making me hitchhike back from miles out of town—not to mention the whole issue of having to rob my brother—if that's how you treat a fan, I'd hate to see what

28

you do to your enemies." I paused and tried to smile, but Seth wasn't having it. I gave up. "Seriously, dude. You went too far."

Seth pulled his lips tight, then turned and allowed Officer Olaf to lead him out of the office. The officer nodded at Principal Gorse on the way out. "Thanks, Hank," he said, glancing briefly at me and my brother. "Boys."

Then he turned his head and walked out the door, and he and Seth were gone.

Principal Gorse sighed. "Sometimes, boys," he said, "I think the world is changing too fast for me. Can either of you explain the appeal of that movie to me? Watching people get scared out of their minds for no real purpose?" He shook his head and shrugged.

"I think it's about shock, sir," I said. "In this day and age we've been desensitized to trauma, crime, horrific happenings. It takes more and more to shock your audience. Look at movies like *Saw* or *Hostel*—they go much further than the classic Hitchcockian horror of the past."

Principal Gorse nodded, looking bemused.

"So the natural next step," I went on, "the final frontier, if you will, is real emotion. Instead of trying to shock his audience, Seth is allowing them to share in the real shock of his unknowing participants."

Principal Gorse blinked. He was a nice guy, really; dressed like he always was, in a slouchy cardigan sweater, along with his usual corduroy pants and brown shoes. He had a kindly face with sort of messy brown hair and glasses. He looked like—well, like a kind of hippieish high school principal. A youngish man, maybe only forty years old, except that he also walked with a fancy hand-carved cane, which was the result of a bad skiing accident five years earlier.

You would probably have been able to pick out Mr. Gorse's car in the teachers' parking lot just by looking at him: It was an orange 1970s Karmann Ghia. Pure beatnik. Even its engine—it made a singular *put-put-put* sound—reminded you of him, so that wherever you were in Bayport, if he was passing anywhere within earshot, you were aware of him through that unique *put-put-put. There goes Mr. Gorse,* you would say to yourself.

We considered Mr. Gorse a friend—he'd been my band teacher in middle school. I knew he liked us. He'd been really nice to Frank and me when the Deal was being negotiated. Now he tilted his head, giving us both a concerned look.

"How are things going, Hardy Boys?" he asked. "I understand the legal problems you boys have had this past year. As a matter of fact, I received a note from the state board of education about you both."

Joe and I shifted uncomfortably in our chairs.

Mr. Gorse opened the letter and started reading. "Apparently, I'm to understand that—as part of a plea agreement with the state attorney general—you are both subject to 'instant recourse.'" He looked up at us. "I guess that's a little bit like probation." He continued reading. "Which, if you are found to engage in any kind of 'independent ama-teur law-enforcement-type activities,' will result in the pair of you being sent to"—here he brought the letter close to his eyes—"the J'Adoube School for Behavior Modification Therapy on Rock Island."

He wasn't telling us anything we didn't know. But it was not pleasant to hear it spoken out loud. "Are you meeting regularly with your legal adviser?" he asked.

Joe and I nodded. Our lawyer was Uncle Ben—Ben Hardy, our dad's brother—a Hartford tax attorney who had been given the thankless job of dealing with all the legal problems we'd accrued in the past year.

"Good. Well, what I wanted to say to you was that all this stuff . . ." He waved at the letter. "It doesn't change anything as far as I'm concerned. The world needs fighters, boys. People with the courage to stand up for what's right. But you can't accomplish your goals if you're locked up in juvenile hall or if your transcripts show half a dozen suspensions. Am I right?"

We nodded.

"Just remember, I'm in your corner. And my door is open, day and night."

Just then, his door actually opened.

"Oh, I'm sorry," a woman said. It was Yukiko Collins, one of the school's art teachers.

Mr. Gorse brightened. It was rumored that he and Ms. Collins were dating. Nobody wanted to pry, on account of

Mr. Gorse being a widower. (His wife had died in the skiing accident that had broken his leg.) But Joe and I liked the idea of Mr. G and Ms. C being an item, because they were our two favorite people at Bayport High.

"That's all right, Ms. Collins," Mr. Gorse said, rising to his feet, a smile on his face. "We were finished here."

As we passed outside, Ms. Collins smiled. She always wore crazy, mismatched clothing with horizontal stripes, and men's hats, and today was no exception.

Everybody loved Ms. Collins. She was one of those teachers who had the knack for always making you feel enthused and entertained. Joe and I had our own reasons for loving her: She had written the recommendation letter that kept us from being sent to the reform school Mr. Gorse had mentioned: J'Adoube—a really notorious place on a tiny, isolated island twenty miles out to sea. All kinds of rumors existed about the place. Rumors about strange "behavior modification therapies" with names like "Swarm" and "Funhouse Mirror." It was also rumored that several kids died each year trying to escape.

Today Ms. Collins seemed troubled. "I hope you boys are careful about talking on your cell phones," she said.

Smiling at this haphazard warning, I said, "You don't believe that stuff about their causing brain cancer, do you, Ms. Collins?"

"No, but I think mine's been hacked or something. . . ."

That sounded odd. I wanted to ask her more about it.

But Mr. Gorse invited her in. She said good-bye to us with that same uneasy air, and the door shut behind them.

In the lobby, Principal Gorse's secretary, Connie, smiled and held up two green late passes. "How's Trudy, boys?"

Connie knew Aunt Trudy from their gardening club. Together, they'd helped make an untended plot in back of the school into an overflowing vegetable garden. The cafeteria even used the fresh veggies in its daily special. (Not that you could tell, really. If only Aunt Trudy would teach some cooking classes down there!)

"She's good," Frank said with a smile. "We'll tell her you say hi."

Connie nodded. "I'd appreciate that. Have a good day, boys."

I'm not sure Connie needed to bother with the late passes. Frank and I both had study hall in the cafeteria next with Coach Gerther, who barely glanced at the passes before grabbing them out of our hands and gesturing vaguely at the rows of tables. "Take a seat."

Coach Gerther was rumored to have lost 80 percent of his hearing in the Vietnam War, which made him the perfect teacher for study hall. The din regularly reached rock-concert levels. It was literally impossible to get any work done in there, unless your "work" involved studying the effects of loud noises on hearing over time. Frank and I settled at a table in the back, and Frank pulled out a notebook.

"So . . . ," he began. "About the speech . . ."

"Yo—Hardy boys!"

I looked up to see Sharelle Bunyan standing over us. Well, *looming* over us was more like it. She was the queen of pep. Although she was an old friend of mine from junior high, we'd drifted apart in high school. She was very popular (not that we were *un*popular—but she was definitely in the alpha group).

It was actually nice to see her. She had the same red curly hair she'd had as a kid, only now she wore her cheerleader uniform, with the Bayport High colors of green and gold and the school mascot—Bill the Bulldog—pictured snarling on the front.

"Hey, Sharelle. Long time no see. What's up?"

"I was hoping," she said, "that you guys would be able to volunteer for the blood drive." She sat down next to us. As she did, she accidentally dropped a clipboard she was carrying. It clattered to the floor. "Shoot!" She picked it up and dusted it off, then held it out under our noses. Apparently, we had no choice but to sign up. "Ball of energy" is how people used to describe her in junior high. I saw that the description was still applicable.

"Um, sure, Sharelle."

"Yeah, we're always happy to bleed for a good cause."

We were starting to add our names to the list when she spoke to us under her breath. As she did, her whole demeanor changed. She sounded panicky.

"Look, guys—I need your help," she whispered. Something about her mood was contagious. We lowered our voices to match hers and kept our heads down.

"What kind of help?" Frank asked.

"You know . . . with a *mystery*."

A mystery. There it was. You have no idea how a reputation as a teenage detective can complicate your life. Frank started to answer, but I gave him a nudge. He picked up on my wariness and stayed silent. The truth was, although it sounded harmless and kind of fun, this wasn't an innocent topic for us anymore. There were serious consequences for us involved with anything remotely connected to sleuthing. Consequences that Frank and I didn't talk about, because . . . well, we didn't like to *think* about them. Not that they would stop us. But we still had to be more careful now than we used to be.

"Why ask us?" I said cautiously.

"Oh, come on," Sharelle said. "Don't give me that. Everybody knows you guys are, like, Sherlock Squared. You're both packing heat, right?"

"Don't believe everything you hear, Sharelle."

"Well, anyway—I need help. Or . . . well, Neal needs help." She was the only person in school who did not refer to her older brother as Neanderthal Bunyan—yes, the same charming fellow who'd introduced Frank to his impending Internet fame this morning. He was also the star linebacker of the BHS football team.

"Is he all right? Did something happen to him?"

"Yes. He's . . . fine, more or less. Physically at least. But . . ."

She glanced around the hall. Clearly, she was uneasy discussing this out in the open. "Look, I'm going to ask for a bathroom pass. Can you guys follow me, and we can talk about it out by the vending machines?" It would be quieter there. Apparently, the blood drive had been a cover story to make contact with us.

She got up to lead us out of the cafeteria. I was cautious but curious. I started to follow her, but Frank said, "We'll meet you there in five."

Sharelle seemed puzzled. She looked like she wanted to say something, but instead she just nodded and walked off.

Frank watched her go up to Coach Gerther, get her pass, and head out the door. Then he turned to me, his expression dark. "Neanderthal Bunyan—asking us for help," he said. "That doesn't seem odd to you?"

The truth was, it did.

It was six or seven months ago—before we had to retire. Joe and I had tracked down a drug ring. What we didn't know or anticipate was the series of busts around town that would follow—the consequences of our investigation, including the arrest of the former star linebacker for the Bayport High School football team, Neal "Neanderthal" Bunyan, all-state three years running, who had apparently been abusing steroids.

Neanderthal Bunyan had good reason to enjoy seeing Frank and me humiliated. Would he even accept our help?

"Let's just be careful," Frank suggested.

It might be a challenge, in some classes, for two brothers to get bathroom passes for simultaneous bathroom trips. But fortunately, Coach Gerther had stopped caring a long time ago, possibly before we were born. He grabbed two passes from a big coffee can he kept on his desk and waved us away.

We found Sharelle waiting where she said she'd be, by the vending machines. Frank and I took a seat on either side of her.

"So what's going on with Neanderthal?" I said.

"Okay," she said in an excited whisper. "This, like, totally *insane* thing has been happening. . . ."

MONITORED 5

FRANK

'M NOT SURE WHO WAS THE LEAST COMFORT-able when Sharelle led Joe and me into Neanderthal Bunyan's bedroom that afternoon. Neanderthal was lying back on his bed, all his attention focused on the football-themed video game he was playing on the TV that hung on the wall.

"Get out, Sharelle," he said without looking up, but when three people walked in, and not one, he sighed, hit a pause button, and looked up.

"Oh," he said, looking startled and not pleased. "It's—"

"You need help, Neal," Sharelle said in a bossy voice. I had a sudden premonition of what it might feel like to have Sharelle as a sister, and a chill ran down my spine. "I asked these guys to come over because I knew you never would."

Neanderthal didn't say anything. He was staring from me to Joe with a curled lip, like he smelled something horrible. "I don't need any help from these two," he said, and picked up the game controller again. He unpaused the game and turned his attention back to the screen. "You can show yourselves out," he finished.

Fair enough. I touched Joe's arm and started heading for the door. We weren't supposed to be doing any investigation right now . . . so why waste time trying to convince a guy who didn't even want our help? But Joe seemed to hesitate, looking to Sharelle. Suddenly she jumped forward, grabbing the controller from her brother's hand.

"HEY!" Neanderthal yelled.

"HEY YOURSELF!" she shouted back, matching him on volume. She gestured to me and Joe. "I asked these guys to come over today because even though you don't have the best history, they're the only ones who can help you," Sharelle finished.

Neanderthal pursed his lips. Clearly, he didn't like the direction of this conversation. But I could tell that Sharelle's words were making a dent. He let out a groan and looked down at his New York Giants comforter. Then he crossed his arms and settled back against the head of his bed, still scowling, still not looking at us.

"Do you want to tell them what happened?" Sharelle asked, moving closer to the bed.

Neanderthal shook his head. "You tell them," he muttered.

Sharelle turned back to face Joe and me. "Okay," she said. "About a week ago, Neal started getting some very weird e-mails."

I nodded slowly. "Weirder than the e-mail this morning with the link to the movie trailer?"

Neanderthal gave me a contemptuous look. "Dude, way weirder than that," he said. "What do I care about you guys getting robbed in some bank? No, this was . . ." He trailed off, staring off into the distance, fear invading his expression.

Not sure how to proceed, I looked to Sharelle. "This was?" I prompted.

Sharelle looked at Neanderthal, as though waiting to see whether he could pull himself together and finish the story. When he didn't move for a few seconds, she sighed and turned back to us. "This was really creepy," she said. "The address was one he didn't recognize, and the e-mail itself was just a link. No signature, no message."

I looked at Joe. This was sounding familiar. "Okay . . . and?"

Sharelle paused and looked at her brother. "Tell them, Neal."

We both turned to face Neal. He was staring at the black television screen, and as we watched, he seemed to shake himself off and looked down at his comforter. "The link went to a video," he said, then swallowed. "The video was . . . it was of me sleeping," he said quickly, then shook his head again.

I looked at Joe. He looked just as confused as I felt. "Sleeping?" he asked. "As in . . ."

"As in right here, in this bed," Neanderthal said, patting

the mattress beneath him. "I don't know when it was taken. Or how. Or by who. But whoever made it . . ." His voice wavered. "They were watching me all night."

I met Joe's eyes. "Wow. That's really . . ."

"Creepy," Joe finished. He shivered a little. "Man, I think I have the willies now."

Neanderthal looked a little relieved. "Yeah?" he asked. "It's freaking me out too. I just don't know who would want to watch me sleep—or why."

"That's not all," Sharelle added.

"It's not?" I asked.

Neanderthal was shaking his head. "No," he said. "The really creepy thing is, it's happened more than once. I've gotten three videos e-mailed to me over the last five days."

I frowned. "So whoever's watching you sleep—they might be doing it a lot."

Neanderthal nodded. "And it looks like—I mean, this really creeps me out, but it looks like you can watch the video feed live on the web. They e-mail me links to the recordings, but there's also a link to watch the live video." He paused. "I just don't get it," he said finally. "I don't know who would want me monitored. I don't think I have any enemies—I mean, besides you guys."

Touché. I looked at Joe.

"Can we see them?" he asked.

Neanderthal looked a little uncomfortable, but he nodded. "Yeah, let me just fire up my computer."

While he walked over to the desk on the left side of the room and opened up a blue laptop, I took a quick scan of the room, looking for anything suspicious and cameralike. Nothing stood out, though. Neanderthal had a surprisingly minimalist decorating style. Whoever had hidden a camera in here must have really tried hard.

After a minute or so, Neanderthal called us over to his computer. He had a web browser open to his e-mail. "Here it is."

He clicked on a message from youreup@fastmail.net. There was no subject, and when the message opened, it contained only a link.

Neanderthal clicked on the link, and a grainy black-and-white video started up.

It took me a minute to figure out what all the shapes were in the dim light, but then I could make out Neanderthal, in his bed, tossing and turning, then lying still.

The video was silent apart from the sound of Neanderthal breathing and the occasional creak of the springs in his mattress.

"Whoa," muttered Joe.

"Have you looked for a camera?" I asked. I turned in the direction the video was shot from; it looked like the camera had been on Neanderthal's shelf of sports trophies.

"That's the really creepy thing," Neanderthal said, clicking back to the web browser and opening up another e-mail. He clicked on that link, and another grainy black-and-white video started up, this one shot from a totally different direction. It looked like this camera had been posted just above his door. What the . . . ?

"Every time I get a video, I look for the camera," Neanderthal explained, "but I never find anything. Not even anything they might have hidden the camera inside. It's like each time they film me, they're sneaking in a camera, then coming back in, taking it out, and . . ."

"And uploading the video and sending you the link," Joe finished.

Neanderthal nodded. "I keep searching my room," he said. "Every night before bed, I look for a camera. But I never find it. Lately . . ." He stopped and rubbed his temples. "Lately the videos start after I'm already asleep. I feel like they're sneaking in . . ."

"While you're sleeping?" I asked. Super creepy!

Neanderthal sighed and nodded. "I can't believe it either," he said. "The last couple nights, I've set my alarm to wake up at one in the morning, and then again at three. I figure I'll get up and check the web, figuring that if the video's running, I can at least find the camera."

I nodded. "And how's that worked out?" I asked.

Neanderthal and Sharelle exchanged a concerned look. "It hasn't," Neanderthal admitted. "I wake up in the morning and find that someone turned off the alarm."

A chill went down my spine. "Wow."

"We tried to set up our own camera the other night," added

Sharelle, "but when we tried to watch the footage, it was two hours of Neal sleeping, and then it just went black. It was like someone disabled the camera without ever being seen."

Joe's mouth was hanging open. "That is . . . wow."

Sharelle turned to me. "We have a burglar alarm," she said. "My parents set it every night when they lock the door, which is hours before Neal goes to bed. It monitors all the doors and windows. But lately we've noticed after each time, the alarm has been turned off somehow."

Joe shook his head and let out a low whistle. "How're they doing it?" he asked.

I looked around the room, then walked over to the windows, giving them a little jiggle. Everything looked really secure.

"Is there anyone outside the family who has the code to the alarm?" I asked.

"No way," Sharelle scoffed. "Mom guards that code with her life. She wouldn't even give it to either of us till we turned sixteen."

I nodded slowly, looking at Joe. He looked just as lost as I felt.

"Okay," I said, trying to gather my wits. "I'm glad you reached out to us, Sharelle, because I think we can help. Here's what we're going to do. . . ."

THE ARROW

6

JOE

I HAVE TO ADMIT THAT I WAS A LITTLE STUNNED when Frank started with the "Here's what we're going to do." Because I had no idea what to do. Whoever was monitoring Neanderthal had reached a level of creepy I had only encountered in horror movies and bad dreams. I was no fan of the guy, but even I had trouble imagining what he could have done to deserve this.

When Frank explained further, though, it started to make sense. Whoever was monitoring Neanderthal was good. Clearly, he—or she—knew how to break into a secure house, plant a camera, feed all the footage to the Internet, and do it all without being caught—despite Neanderthal and Sharelle both knowing that this was going on.

It didn't make sense to try to beat that person at their

own game. As Frank explained, all we could do, for now, was try to observe the monitor.

I yawned as Frank fired up his laptop and got on the web.

"Really?" Frank asked, smirking. "Already? It's ten o'clock."

I shook my head. "That was a stress-relief yawn," I said. "I'm tense. Animals yawn to release tension."

Frank looked skeptical. "Either way, maybe I should take the first shift while you take a nap."

I blinked, watching the screen as Frank opened up the e-mail that Neanderthal had forwarded to us and clicked on the link. Nothing was up yet—just a big black box that said WATCH FOR COMING ATTRACTIONS!

"I can watch with you for a while," I said, making myself comfortable with some pillows on Frank's bed. "So hey . . . do you think Seth Diller is involved in this?"

Frank frowned as he stared at the screen. "That was my first thought too," he admitted. "It just seems like too much of a coincidence. Neanderthal comes to us about this strange, video-related trouble, the same day that . . ."

"Seth Diller gets arrested for causing trouble with his video camera," I finished.

Frank nodded grimly. "But it seems a little . . ." He paused, searching for the right word.

"Sophisticated?" I suggested. Seth's movies were endlessly entertaining . . . but sophisticated they were not.

Frank sighed. "I was going to say sinister," he finished.

That made me sit up. "Sinister?" I asked. "You don't think making me commit a felony and then kidnapping me was sinister?"

"Seth knows you," Frank explained, and at my incredulous expression, added, "Well, a little bit. He knew you could handle what he was dishing out."

"And Neanderthal?" I asked. Neanderthal had never struck me as a delicate flower.

Frank shivered. "This is just creepier. I don't know that anyone could handle what he's getting."

I didn't say anything to that. After a few seconds I yawned again.

Frank didn't lift his eyes from the computer. "I don't know. Might be torture to watch someone sleep while you're sleepy yourself."

"I don't know what you're talking about," I said. "I'm very perky."

Frank snorted, and then the black box on the screen suddenly filled in with the darkened image of Neanderthal's room. Neanderthal lay in a big lump on the left side of his double bed. The comforter was pulled up to his chin, and his breathing was regular. But there was something off about him. He looked weirdly stiff.

"He's awake," I said.

"Wouldn't you be?" Frank asked.

Well, yeah. It actually impressed me that Neanderthal was getting any sleep at all these days. I would have a really hard time forgetting that someone was about to break into my room and broadcast my sleeping form on the Web. You'd have to count a lot of sheep to fall asleep under those circumstances, I figured. I thought of my own tried-and-true trick to get myself to sleep: counting, naming, and picturing the crooks Frank and I had put away, one by one, starting from the earliest and moving on toward the most recent. There was Bruce Fishkill, the kid who'd stolen the class hamster in first grade. Nasty little kid—and I know it's not nice to call children nasty but really, this kid was something else. When we went out for recess after it rained, he would run around stomping on all the worms who'd been flooded out of their holes. And that still doesn't even come close to what he did to Jeannie Gilbright's chocolate milk that one time. . . .

"Joe. JOE!"

I was startled awake by a swift kick from my brother.

"Not in the milk!" I mumbled, blinking and shaking my head.

Frank was pointing at the computer screen. "Get serious, bro. We've got action here."

I swiped the backs of my hands over my eyes and sat up, feeling dizzy. Frank was pointing at the picture of Neanderthal sleeping—and he did really seem to be sleeping now.

"What's up?" I asked. "I don't see any—OH, CRAP!"

My brother and I have seen a lot of things, and generally, I think you'll find, we're pretty unflappable. But sometimes you see something and the only proper human response is OH, CRAP!

Like when you're watching live video of one of your classmates sleeping and a figure dressed all in black, and wearing one of those rubber Halloween masks—Jay Leno, I think—suddenly pops into the bottom right corner of the image and waves at the camera.

"What is he doing?" I asked, thinking out loud. I have a nasty habit of doing that when I'm under stress. "What is he doing there? Is he going to—OH, CRAP!"

Another figure appeared in the bottom left corner, this one wearing a Conan O'Brien mask, and also waved. Then they both turned and started advancing toward Neanderthal.

Frank grabbed his phone off his nightstand. "That's it. I'm calling the police."

I didn't argue.

"I thought this was a prank," I said as Frank dialed 911. "It was creepy, sure, but I thought it was harmless."

The moment the word "harmless" left my mouth, Jay Leno grabbed Neanderthal's sleeping form, lifted him from the pillow, and—*BLAM!*—punched him in the face.

Frank's mouth dropped open. "Oh my— Hello? Yes, I'm calling to report a break-in and assault at 83 Hillside Drive. . . ."

There was no sound in the video, but Neanderthal was definitely awake now, and I could see him let out a scream before Conan pulled out a few inches of duct tape and stuck it over his mouth.

Together, Jay and Conan pulled Neanderthal off the bed. He was out of frame, but I could see the two masked intruders railing back to punch him again.

Frank was finishing up his call. "Okay. Okay, then. Thank you."

He clicked off his phone and looked at me. His expression was serious. "They're sending the police." Then he reached over to his desk and grabbed the car keys.

"Let's go save a football player," he said grimly.

A police cruiser was already sitting in the Bunyans' driveway when we arrived, lights flashing.

Frank and I jumped out of the car and ran up to the front door. Through the window, we could see quite the little convention gathered in the brightly lit living room: Sharelle, her mother, two officers . . . but I didn't see Neanderthal.

A big, burly man with wild gray hair and a bushy mustache pulled open the door and regarded us suspiciously. "You two called the police?" he demanded, in a not-exactly-grateful tone.

The door behind him swung open another inch, and I could see Neanderthal standing there. He was okay! He had a black eye and he looked—well—uncomfortable, but he was still standing.

Frank nodded. "Yes, sir. Neander—Neal asked for our

help with his problem, and we saw that someone had broken into his room. I called the police right away."

Neal's father let out a snort and walked away. *So much for gratitude,* I thought.

Actually, I realized as I scanned the room, nobody looked exactly happy to see us. Least of all Officer Olaf, who was standing next to his new partner—a rookie—and frowning at us.

"Neal here seems to think you overreacted," Officer Olaf said, tapping the tip of his pen against his notebook. "He says what you witnessed was some sort of football team prank. Right, Neal?"

We turned to face Neal, who was wearing a fleecy blue robe with flannel pants and looked supremely uncomfortable. "That's right," he said, but he wasn't quite meeting my eyes—or Frank's. He was looking past us, at the wall behind our heads. He made a face and shrugged. "It was a joke. You know, no big deal. The guys took off when they heard the police. They were really freaked."

Frank looked at Officer Olaf. "And you didn't chase them?"

Olaf glared at him. "Your friend here seems to think no crime was committed," he says. "The window was open. His friends snuck in to play a prank."

Instinctively, I turned to Sharelle. She was looking at her big brother, concerned, but she wouldn't meet my eyes either (or Frank's). I glanced at my brother, who looked just as confused as I felt. What was going on here?

Frank cleared his throat. "Well, gosh, we're sorry to waste everyone's time," he said, staring daggers at Neanderthal. "We sure could've sworn we witnessed a violent assault on Neal that was broadcast over the Internet. But maybe we were misinterpreting."

Neanderthal still wouldn't look at Frank. He crossed his arms in front of his chest and looked at the carpet.

I had an idea. "Hey, Neal, I think I left my phone in your room when we were here earlier," I said. "You wouldn't mind taking us back there so I can grab it? Maybe you can explain what happened, too."

Officer Olaf sighed deeply and shoved his notebook at his rookie partner. "Gosh!" he said, clearly mocking us. "Oh, golly gee! We're the Hardy Boys, and we sure are sorry to waste the taxpayers' time and money." He stomped toward us and paused to glare at my brother, then me. "Typical," he muttered, shaking his head. "When are you two going to learn to mind your own business?"

He stomped past us, out the door. His rookie partner looked befuddled, then smiled nervously at everyone and followed him. "Um, good night. Sorry to barge in on you all."

Neanderthal nodded at Frank and started walking down the hall toward his room. We both followed. Behind us, Neanderthal's parents looked at each other, shrugged, and started turning off the lights.

Once we were back in Neanderthal's room, I closed the

door behind us. "You want to explain to us what the heck just happened?"

Neanderthal sighed. He moved around his bed, picking a pair of socks up off his floor and throwing them into his hamper. "I'm sorry you guys misunderstood," he said quietly.

"Misunderstood?" said Frank. He stepped forward. "Neal, come on. We agreed to help you, and you just made fools of us." He paused and looked around the room. "Where's the camera? Or did they take it back?"

Neanderthal didn't answer. He was rubbing his shoulder thoughtfully. His eyes kept going to this one spot on the floor.

"Are you hurt?" I asked. He wasn't obviously bleeding or anything, but Jay and Conan might have done all kinds of damage before the police showed up.

Neal shook his head. "I told you," he said. "It was just a joke. No big deal."

I could tell that my normally coolheaded brother was starting to get frustrated. "Was this some kind of warped revenge thing?" he asked, moving closer. "Is that it? Because—"

Suddenly Frank reached out and yanked down the sleeve of Neanderthal's robe. Neanderthal jumped and grabbed at the sleeve, but not before we saw his shoulder and the top of his arm—which were covered in bruises.

"Neal!" I cried, moving closer. "That doesn't look like my idea of a joke."

Neanderthal backed away, yanking his robe back on and

53

crossing his arms. "You guys, come on. I think you should leave."

"Not before you explain what's going on," Frank insisted. He lowered his voice. "Why are you lying?" he asked. "What really happened tonight? You can tell us."

Neanderthal didn't respond, just stared at the floor and shook his head. After a few seconds of silence—during which we didn't leave—he finally raised his eyes to meet Frank's.

They were full of fear.

"Please," he said finally, in a low voice. "If you know what's good for you—or me—you will forget that Sharelle ever asked you here. It was a misunderstanding, okay? I don't need your help."

Frank frowned, then turned to me. I shook my head, mystified. What could it take to scare Neanderthal Bunyan—one of the biggest meatheads in school—this badly?

"Okay," I said after a minute or so. "We'll take your word for it, Neal. If you want us to leave, we'll leave."

I looked at Frank and raised my eyebrows, like, *Shall we?* Personally, I was done trying to make nice with Neanderthal. Obviously, something was going on with him. But if he didn't want to tell us about it, so be it.

Frank hesitated before nodding. Before he moved, though, he turned back to Neanderthal and lowered his voice. "If you ever want to tell us what's really going on," he said, "we're here."

Clearly, Frank has more patience than I do. I was already fantasizing about my nice warm bed and the four or so hours of sleep I could still get if we hightailed it home. But when we turned to walk out the door, something jumped out at me.

It was right over Neal's bedroom door—just above the center of the door frame.

A tiny red triangle with what looked like little legs coming out of it. Painted on, like with a stencil.

It definitely hadn't been there when Frank and I had come by earlier.

In fact, it was shiny. Was the paint still wet?

I pointed. "Neal—what the heck is that?"

Neal's reaction was brief but intense. His face turned scarlet and his eyes widened like a ghost had appeared behind us. But then he looked down at the floor and shook his head, and when he faced us again, he looked totally nonchalant.

"What do you mean?" he asked. "That red thing? Just something stupid Sharelle and I painted up there when I was little."

Frank stared at the symbol. "I could swear that wasn't there be—"

But Neal kept talking, drowning him out. "We were into Native Americans. Arrowheads. You know."

He walked around his bed toward us, then opened the door and raised his voice. "Well, bye now. You two sleep well."

My brother and I regarded each other warily. Neanderthal's parents could clearly hear us now. No way he was going to reveal anything else.

"Okay," I said, strolling through the door. "Well, good night."

Frank didn't look terribly eager to leave, but it was clear he got the message too. We walked down the hallway to the living room and the front door. As we were about to leave, a figure jumped up off the couch in the darkened room, startling us.

Sharelle.

She walked over, not quite meeting our eyes. "Good night, guys," she said, and then, lowering her voice so only we could hear her, "Sorry."

Frank leaned closer and lowered his voice to match hers. "I don't suppose you want to tell us what's really going on?" he whispered.

Sharelle looked up at him. Her eyes were full of regret. "See you around," she said, in her normal tone.

I sighed. "Right," I said, walking through the door behind my brother and closing it behind us. "See you around."

PANIC PROJECT 7

FRANK

DON'T KNOW ABOUT JOE, BUT I DIDN'T GET much sleep when we finally got home from our aborted attempt to save Neanderthal Bunyan's life. Something about the way he'd looked at me—*If you know what's good for you, or me*—with his eyes full of fear. It was an emotion I normally didn't associate with football players. It just creeped me out.

In the morning, as I drove to school, Joe suddenly piped up. "It was revenge," he said decisively.

"What?"

"The whole deal at Neanderthal's house last night," he said. He was looking out the window thoughtfully, watching Main Street fly by. "It has to be some cockamamie plot of his to get revenge for being put away somehow, I've decided."

I snorted. "Well, if you've decided, it must be true," I said sarcastically.

Joe turned away from the window. He looked stung.

"Sorry," I said. "I'm just not so convinced."

"What else could it be?" Joe asked, holding out his hands in a beseeching gesture. "I've run though everything in my head. The Mafia. Zombies. Killer robots."

"I think it could be killer robots," I muttered, pulling into the parking lot. But he wasn't paying attention, which was sort of why I'd said it. I didn't think there were killer robots. In Bayport.

"Unless you believe there's a force out there that could scare Neanderthal Bunyan into total submission," Joe went on, "which I don't . . . the only logical explanation is revenge."

I pulled the car into our usual parking space, put it in park, and turned off the engine. Neither one of us made any move to get out of the car just yet.

"It could be Seth Diller," I said finally.

Joe wrinkled his nose. "Pfft," he said. "Seth Diller."

I looked at him. "You were the one who thought he was sinister enough to pull this off."

Joe was staring out the windshield now. "That was before last night," he said.

"Before the beating?" I clarified.

"Before I saw Neanderthal Bunyan with the poop scared out of him," he corrected me.

I looked out the windshield. A bunch of freshman cheerleaders were running around with "spirit boxes" they'd made for the football players. They contained cookies, usually. I noticed Sharelle among them, carrying a shoe box decorated in the BHS colors. Maybe it was just me, but it looked like some of the pep had been sucked out of her. She seemed to walk a little more slowly and carefully, like something was pressing her down from above.

Maybe Neanderthal's situation—whatever it was—was weighing as heavily on her as it was on us.

"We should still talk to Seth when he's back," I said, unbuckling my seat belt and grabbing my backpack. The first bell was going to ring in three minutes. It occurred to me that since the bank "robbery," I'd made absolutely no progress on my speech.

Detective work and schoolwork never mixed well. Which was part of the reason for the Deal.

Joe sighed and unbuckled his seat belt. "Great," he said, taking his turn at sarcasm. "I'm sure Seth will be really psyched to talk to us."

"Hey, Seth."

Joe and I had caught up with our favorite prankster in the hot-food line in the cafeteria. When he was back three days later, he seemed to be torn between the ravioli and the meatballs.

"Go for the special of the day," Joe advised. His tray was already piled high with it.

Seth looked at both of us like he'd just lost his appetite. He looked at Joe's tray and his expression worsened. "What is it?" he asked Joe.

Joe looked down. "Mostly peas," he replied neutrally.

Seth sighed and shook his head, turning back to the line. "Ravioli, please," he asked the lady behind the trays.

"Bad choice," Joe said, looking disappointed. "Did you hear about when Winnie Maxwell found a tooth in her ravioli?"

Seth grimaced. "A human tooth?"

Joe looked at him frankly. "Does it matter?"

We had made it to the cashier now, and Seth paid first, then promptly tried to lose us by running off to a table in the back. The Hardy Boys are pretty quick with cash, though. We paid and were able to catch up to Seth within seconds.

"We need to talk to you," I said, not interested in wasting any more time.

Seth looked straight ahead. "I'm not interested in talking to you," he replied.

"Come on," said Joe. "In my opinion, you still owe me for making me walk all the way home from where that police cruiser dropped me off."

Seth glared at him. "And in my opinion, you can never repay me for making me spend four hours in jail last night."

Four hours? What an amateur. "What, your parents wouldn't pick you up?"

Seth sighed and nodded. "My dad is not talking to me this century," he said. "As of yesterday. Thanks to you."

"Really, thanks to you, Seth," I pointed out. "As I have mentioned before, you did kind of rob a bank."

"And as I have mentioned before," Seth replied, "it was a harmless prank."

Hmm. The three of us had reached the end of the cafeteria, but stubbornly, Seth made no move to sit down, probably not wanting to invite a long conversation. I gestured to the table behind us. "Shall we?"

But Seth shook his head deliberately back and forth, like a kindergartener. "Can you just say what you need to say and we'll be done with it?"

Joe was frowning, thinking about something. "Hey, how did you get access to the cruiser?" he asked.

"What?"

"The police cruiser," he clarified. "For your little harmless prank."

Seth raised his chin defiantly. "I know people."

Interesting. "What kind of people?" I asked.

"Important people," Seth replied. "City people."

"And they were willing to go along with your dangerous prank?" I asked. "Who was this?"

"I'll never tell," Seth replied. "I protect my allies. Look, can we get to the point?"

I glanced at Joe. "Neal Bunyan," I said simply.

Automatically, Seth's eyes went to the table toward the front where the football players—even former ones like Neanderthal—always sat. But Neal wasn't there today. He hadn't come to school. I wasn't sure whether to be worried about that.

Seth looked confused. "What about him?"

I put my tray down on the nearest table, pulled out my phone, and went into my e-mail. I still had the message Neanderthal had forwarded to me the day before, with the link to the video footage. I clicked on it and held it up for Seth. "See that?"

Seth squinted, then frowned. "Is that Neal?" he asked. "Sleeping?"

"Someone's been breaking into his house to film him sleeping and broadcast it on the Web," Joe explained.

"What? Why?" said Seth.

"I don't know," I said, giving Seth an accusing look. "Why?"

"Wha-what are you . . . ?" Seth looked down at the video again. "Why would I want to film Neal Bunyan sleeping?"

Joe leaned closer, lowering his voice. "Maybe so that when a couple of masked goons broke into his bedroom last night and beat him up, you'd get the whole thing on video."

Seth stared at Joe, stunned. "What?"

"Tell us the truth, Seth," I said, leaning in. "Is this part of the Panic Project? Are you hoping we'll see Neal's beating on the big screen someday?"

Seth looked at my phone, horrified, and shook his head. "No!" he insisted. "Look, we might disagree about the bank heist prank, but I would never plan a prank for Panic Project that involved someone really getting hurt."

"How do we know you're telling the truth?" Joe asked.

"Well, for one," Seth said, "I was at the police station until midnight last night, and then my parents took me right home." He paused. "As you might imagine, they were keeping a pretty close eye on me. I think they'll vouch for me being home all night."

Hmm. The beating had started a little after midnight. Admittedly, it would be pretty hard for Seth to get out of jail, put on black clothes and a mask, and run to Neal Bunyan's house to beat him up.

But Joe looked less than convinced. "That doesn't mean you couldn't have gotten someone else to do it," he pointed out. "Maybe one of the important people you know?"

He had a point. "What else have you got?" I asked.

Seth sighed. "I—I—" He stopped and looked at the screen on my phone. The video had stopped. He put his tray down, reached over, and restarted the video. Then he smiled and pointed. "Aha!"

"Aha?" asked Joe.

"That's not my camera," Seth said, pointing at the video. "It's way higher quality video than the one I have. This was made with a pretty expensive camera. See?"

He pulled out his own phone and played the bank robber video. Indeed, it was much grainier and less sharp than the video of Neal.

But Joe still looked skeptical. "That doesn't mean you only have one camera," he said.

Seth sighed. "Look," he said, pulling up his website on his phone. "Watch any video. Any movie I've made. I guarantee you, none of them will match the picture on this video."

We clicked through a few. Seth was right. Some of the video quality was better than his phone's, but none of them were as sharp as the video of Neanderthal.

"And how do we know you didn't buy this camera especially for the Neal project?" Joe asked. But I could tell from his tone that his heart wasn't in it. Seth had convinced him.

"That's, like, a thousand-dollar camera," Seth replied. "You can ask my parents. For real, I don't have that kind of money. If I was saving up for a camera like that, they'd know."

I looked at Joe. I could tell we were both thinking the same thing: Seth was telling the truth.

"Okay," Joe said finally. "We believe you. I guess the Panic Project is dead."

"As a doornail," said Seth bitterly. "Thanks to you guys."

"But let me ask you something." Joe put his tray down and grabbed his napkin. Then he pulled a pencil out from behind his ear—a Joe-ism, to make sure he always has something to write with in school—and sketched something on the napkin. "Do you know what this symbol is?"

Joe held up the napkin and I swear, Seth paled visibly. I grabbed the napkin to get a look myself and realized that it was the triangle-with-legs symbol we'd seen over Neal's door last night. Or early this morning, technically.

Seth seemed to pull himself together with effort. "Nope," he said finally. "Anything else?"

"You sure you've never seen that symbol before?" I asked, pointing at the napkin. "This one right here?"

Seth swallowed hard and shook his head. "Nope. Well, gotta go."

"Never?" asked Joe, seeming to pick up on Seth's reaction too.

Seth looked from Joe to me, his expression squirrelly. He was kind of a squirrelly guy in general, but this was a particularly squirrelly moment. "You guys have never seen that symbol before?" he asked.

"What does that mean?" Joe asked.

"What does what mean?" asked Seth. He gave an exaggerated shrug. "Where did you see it?"

"Over Neal's bedroom door," I said.

Recognition sparked in Seth's eyes, as if what we were telling him suddenly made sense. But just as quickly as it appeared, Seth buried it. "Well, I don't know what it is," he repeated. "Look, if you'll excuse me, I want to eat my ravioli now." He picked up his tray, and before Joe or I could decide whether to stop him, took off in the direction of the AV room.

SECRETS 8

JOE

"YOU SAW IT, RIGHT?" I ASKED MY BROTHER as we finally settled down at the table in the back of the cafeteria with our food. My peas were cold.

"What am I, blind?" asked Frank, poking at his turkey sandwich. Frank has this inexplicable distaste for the hot food in the cafeteria. He doesn't know what he's missing, in my opinion. "Of course I saw it. He was scared. The minute you showed him that symbol, whatever it is, he got scared."

I forked a few more peas, then tapped them against the tray. I was about to respond when Janine Kornbluth walked by on her way out of the cafeteria. When she saw me, she smiled and gave a little wave. I stared after her, unable to pull myself together enough to wave back.

I'll admit it wasn't the first time I'd been distracted by the thought of Janine Kornbluth. I'd noticed her a few weeks ago, her dark hair and pale face with the little crease between her eyebrows that meant she was thinking. We were in the same French class. I liked how quietly she did everything. Right down to the way she closed her locker, which she did quietly, instead of slamming it like I always did.

Good sense told me she was completely out of my league. I was too noisy, for one thing. But still, there had to be some way I could "sell her" on Joe Hardy. Although the perfect idea hadn't occurred to me yet, I was actively brainstorming.

"Joe?" Frank was saying. "JOE? HELLO?"

"Right. Sure. Triangle with legs," I responded, hoping he hadn't totally changed the subject and started talking about electrons or something. (This was Frank, after all.)

Frank looked amused. I was pretty sure he'd seen Janine pass by. "So we'll take a cab ride this afternoon," he said, and took a sip of lemonade.

Cab ride. Oh, *right*. "Sure," I said.

A cab ride was definitely in order to get to the bottom of this whole triangle business.

After school, Frank and I parked the car near the bus station, then hoofed it over to the cab stand. Bayport's bus station is not exactly a metropolitan hub, so it was quiet, between buses, and Frank and I were the only ones waiting for a cab. We had to wave away a couple (that is a surefire way to annoy a cabbie, by the way) before the cab we were looking for, from the Red Apple fleet, medallion number N567, pulled up to the curb.

Frank slid into the backseat, and I followed.

"One conference fare, please," Frank said as I slammed the door behind us.

The driver pulled the cab back onto Main Street, then drove slowly out of the downtown area, toward the more woodsy part of town where houses were few and far between.

"What can I help you boys with?" Professor Al-Hejin said after about ten minutes.

Professor Al-Hejin has been a trusted friend and confidant to Frank and me since we were just starting out this investigation thing. As a full-time cabdriver, the prof hears all the town's most salacious dirt. He knows everything about everything in Bayport. And he's usually willing to share it with Frank and me, because he knows we'll use it for good.

"If I show you a symbol," I said, "can you tell me if you've ever seen it before?"

Professor Al-Hejin met my eyes in the rearview mirror, thoughtful. "I believe so," he said. "Shall I pull over so you can hand it to me?"

I nodded. He pulled into the driveway of an abandoned house, as though he was going to turn around, then idled near the overgrown lawn. I pulled out my triangle-with-legs sketch from lunch that day and passed it through the glass divider to the prof.

Professor Al-Hejin held the napkin up so he could see it. He made no reaction at all. He didn't jump, or gasp, or turn around. In the rearview mirror we could see that his eyes were serious, completely focused on the drawing.

After a few seconds he took his hand off the wheel and very carefully folded the drawing in half. He handed it back to me through the divider, sketch on the inside, not meeting my eyes.

He put the cab in gear and was back on the road, headed back into town, before I could get the question out.

"Professor Al-Hejin? What is it?"

He didn't answer for a few seconds. I could see that his expression was grave, his mouth pulled into a tight line. "I will drop you back off at the bus station," he said quietly.

"What? Why?" asked Frank.

Silence. The woods whizzed by.

"Professor Al-Hejin, please talk to us," I begged as we drew closer to town.

More silence. I looked at Frank, and he looked as confused as I felt. What was going on?

"Professor Al-Hejin," said Frank, "if we insulted you, we didn't mean to. We're just trying to figure out what this symbol means."

"We have no idea," I added.

Professor Al-Hejin remained silent. After a few seconds, though, he pulled over to the side of the road. He sat still for a moment before catching my eye in the rearview mirror.

"Where did you see this symbol?"

I leaned forward. "Over the doorway to our friend's bedroom," I replied.

He looked stung, like that was terrible news. He shook his head, reached into his shirt pocket, pulled out a handkerchief, and wiped his forehead.

Frank and I were quiet for a while, wanting to give him whatever time he needed.

Finally he cleared his throat. "This is a bad symbol," he said simply.

"But what does it mean?" Frank asked.

The prof just shook his head. "Bad men," he said.

"What bad men?" I asked.

Professor Al-Hejin sighed loudly and took his foot off the brake. Within seconds we were back on the road to town.

"Professor," I pleaded as we sailed past factories and warehouses, "whatever you know, you can tell us. Whatever you're afraid of, we don't know anything about."

"We're just hoping to find out what the symbol means," Frank added, "so we can help our friend."

Professor Al-Hejin seemed to think that over. After a minute or so, he looked in the rearview mirror again. "Do you know what it means," he said quietly, "to be marked?"

"Marked, like, for punishment?" I asked. "For death or—I don't know—"

"Your friend is marked," the professor said, just as quietly. "You had best steer clear of him."

I met Frank's eye: *What?*

"How do you know about being marked?" Frank asked. "Were you marked?"

The cab jerked as Professor Al-Hejin suddenly pulled into a gas station. He pulled up to the convenience store and hit the brakes.

"You get out here," he said simply.

I looked at Frank. I had never seen the professor like this. He usually answered all our questions without hesitation. He knew us.

But now I didn't even think it was worth arguing. I'd never seen the professor so spooked.

"Okay," said Frank. He dug a few of Aunt Trudy's famous homemade health bars—these were cranberry with cashews and sesame seeds—out of a pocket in his backpack and handed them through the divider. The prof never let us pay him for the ride. But we liked to give him something for his time and trouble.

Now he hesitated, looking at the bars, then out the window. Frank pushed them forward again, as if to say, *Take them.*

"Please," Frank said. "I'm sorry if we made you uncomfortable."

Professor Al-Hejin slowly took the bars, then caught Frank's eye in the mirror and nodded.

"Bye, Prof," I said, opening my door and scooting out.

The professor nodded again and bit into one of the health

bars. As soon as Frank got out and shut the door behind him, the cab pulled off.

"I guess we're walking back to the station," I said, watching the cab disappear.

"I guess so," said Frank. "Good thing we're only a mile or two away."

I nodded. Slowly we made our way out of the gas station and started walking down the street in the direction of downtown.

"So what do you think?" I asked after a few minutes. We'd both been silent, lost in our own thoughts.

"I think," Frank said, looking serious, "that whatever this is, it's a lot bigger and more dangerous than what happened to Neanderthal."

THE DARK SIDE

9

FRANK

MY BROTHER AND I HAVE ALWAYS HAD kind of a Don't Ask, Don't Tell policy with our father about investigation, or at least we did up until the Deal went into effect. We never told him about cases we were investigating, nor did we ask for his help or advice based on his years of experience as one of the area's top detectives. In return, he never grilled us about how, exactly, we were spending all our free time, or whether we were breaking any laws to do whatever it was we were doing.

As Joe and I returned from our Cab Ride to Nowhere, however, we were both feeling like it might be time to get some advice from Dad. He was nothing if not plugged into the town of Bayport. If this triangle with legs really was as sinister as the professor had implied to us, surely Fenton Hardy had run across it at some point during his career.

When we got home, my mom was in the kitchen, frowning at some photos of a house she was getting ready to show. "No, no, no!" she was saying, circling things in the photo with a black Sharpie. "Not enough lighting! Too much clutter! People, get your shoes into a closet!"

"Got a tough one on your hands, Mom?" Joe asked gently. We Hardys all seem to be Serious about Something. Dad is Serious about the Law. Aunt Trudy is Serious about Food. Joe and I are Serious about Justice. And Mom is Serious about Real Estate.

Mom looked up with a smile. "Boys!" she said. "How have you been? Is your friend feeling better today?"

We'd told our parents that we left in the middle of the night to check on a classmate who'd been in a car accident and was rushed to the hospital. Broken leg, concussion, nothing serious.

"Yeah, great," Joe said. "Already hobbling around on crutches. Hey, Mom, is Dad around?"

Mom gestured to his study. "In his study with the door closed," she replied. "He's been in there all day. Says he's wrestling with a chapter on the Articles of Confederation. It's fighting back, I'm afraid."

Great. So Dad would be in a terrific mood. "Thanks, Mom." I gave her a quick kiss on the cheek, and Joe and I walked over to Dad's study and knocked on the door.

"Come in!" Dad's tone was smack in the middle between

Leave me alone and *Oh please, please, come in here and distract me from this horrible mess.*

"Hi, Dad," I said, pushing open the door and walking in with Joe behind me. Dad was sitting behind his desk, his shirt rumpled, his hair looking like he'd recently been trying to tear it out. (He doesn't have much, either, so that's just an indication of how tough this chapter must have been.)

"Boys," he said, sighing and leaning back in his chair. "Oh, why did I decide to make my career in writing? What demons were possessing me?"

Joe and I were silent. Actually, our dad had left his long career as a detective and taken up writing as part of the Deal. So arguably, the demons in question were Joe and me.

Which didn't exactly make us feel great.

"Dad," I said, deciding to get to the point, "I think Joe and I need to ask you something."

Dad looked at me, suddenly serious. I don't think we'd come in to "ask him something" in a long time . . . probably not since the legal troubles we'd had leading up to the Deal. He sat up straight in his chair, pushing his mouse and keyboard away.

"Sounds serious," he said. "What is it, boys?"

I looked at Joe and nodded. Slowly, he pulled out the napkin he'd sketched the triangle-with-legs symbol on and unfolded it, then pushed it to my father's side of the desk. Dad looked down at it, recognition dawning on his face and then, just as quickly, fear.

"Where did you boys get this?" he demanded in a tight voice.

I cleared my throat, suddenly nervous. "We saw it painted on the wall at a friend's house."

Dad took in a breath, and relief seemed to wash over his face. He grabbed the napkin, balled it up, and threw it in the wastebasket under his desk. "Then this is not something to concern yourselves with."

I looked at Joe. *What?*

"What if we think it's . . . um . . . causing problems for a friend?" Joe asked.

"Who is this friend?" Dad asked, turning his Detective Laser Gaze on my brother. "What has he—or she—gotten himself involved in?"

"Does it matter?" I asked, and then instantly regretted it when the Laser Gaze was pointed at me. I cleared my throat and then continued, more gently, "Is this symbol . . . is it a punishment of some kind? Does it mean someone's marked you?"

Dad sat back in his chair and sighed. He ran his hands through his hair, making it stick up more. "Every town has its dark side," he said, looking up at the ceiling and then back at us. "Why are you asking? What's going on with you boys? You're not investigating again, are you?"

"Of course not," Joe said quickly, reflexively.

I shook my head. "We understand the Deal," I said, not meeting Dad's eye.

"It's just . . ." Joe sat forward in his chair, beseeching Dad.

"This friend of ours. Bad things are happening to him, and he doesn't know why. Is it because of this mark?"

Dad leveled his gaze at Joe, his face neutral. "It could be," he said quietly. Then louder: "Listen, boys, under the circumstances, and with the troubles you're already facing, it is extremely important not to let it get around town that you're asking questions about this . . . this issue. Okay?"

"You mean the triangle with legs?" Joe asked.

"The wha—?" Our father stopped himself and laughed, seeming to get it. Then, just as quickly as it had appeared, the smile was gone. "I'm serious, boys. This is very, very serious business. Some things are best left alone. Uninvestigated. Do you understand? And one of those things is the Red Arrow."

Joe looked at me. *The Red Arrow,* he mouthed. So the triangle with legs had a name.

And our father knew it. And didn't want to talk about it.

Which, for Fenton Hardy, was pretty unusual.

"But, Dad, if the Red Arrow exists," I said, "and it's that terrible—so terrible that no one can even hear you talking about it—shouldn't someone do something about it?"

Dad looked at me. Hoo-boy. This look was even worse than the Laser Gaze. This was the Son, I'm Disappointed in You, But I'm Going to Let My Eyes Do the Talking Gaze.

"Well, Son," he said calmly, "you're assuming that someone hasn't already tried."

I took that in. My mind was reeling with questions: Does

that mean . . . ? Is he saying . . . ? But before I could decide whether even one of them was safe to ask, we were interrupted by loud, tinny music.

"Hit me baby one more time . . . !"

Joe sat up and reached into his pants pocket, yanking out his phone. "I like the classics," he told me sheepishly as he clicked the talk button. "Hello? Yeah, this is he . . . Yeah . . . No, that's . . . Oh no. Oh, man. Okay. Yes."

He clicked off the phone and looked up at Dad and me. "Um," he said awkwardly, "well, thanks, Dad, and point taken. Listen, I think I need to talk to Frank."

Dad nodded and waved us out of his study. "All right, I need to get back to this chapter. Remember what I said, boys."

We assured him that we would and stepped out of the study. Joe closed the door behind us and turned to me with a frantic expression.

"That was Sharelle," he whispered urgently. "Neal was hit by a car today. He's in the hospital!"

BLAST FROM THE PAST

10

JOE

HOSPITALS ARE NOT HAPPY PLACES UNDER the best of circumstances, but when we spotted Sharelle in the lobby of the Bayport Memorial ER, we knew something big was up. Her face was streaked with mascara-y tears, and she was clinging to her cell phone like it was her only friend in the world.

"Frank! Joe!" she cried when she saw us come in. We ran over to her.

"What's going on?" Frank asked urgently.

Sharelle shook her head. "Oh, gosh," she breathed, closing her eyes. A couple more tears squeezed out of the corners, following the trails down her cheeks. "I don't know exactly, except that Neal was hit by a car downtown. It was going fast for the city, and he was unconscious when he came in. The hospital called our house, and I was the only one home. My parents are on their way from work in the city. The doctors are working on Neal now." She paused, then swallowed and squeaked, "I hope he's okay."

"I'm sure he will be, Sharelle," I said, putting my arm around her. I didn't know at all, of course, but I know a person who needs comfort when I see one. I glanced at Frank over Sharelle's head. His expression was as grim as I felt.

Someone had hit Neal with a car? After he'd gotten beat up last night? It couldn't be a coincidence.

We sat down in the uncomfortable plastic chairs that every hospital must buy from the same catalog. Sharelle was sniffling, digging soggy tissues out of her pocket and swiping at her eyes. Frank pulled a handkerchief—yeah, a handkerchief, he gets it from our dad—out of his pocket and handed it to her. Sharelle thanked him and pressed it to the corners of her eyes.

"Sharelle," Frank said in what I knew was his gentlest tone, "can you tell us what really happened last night?"

Sharelle sobbed, pressing the handkerchief to her eyes and then slowly, with shuddering breaths, calming herself. "I'm so sorry, you guys," she said, looking up at Frank and then me. "I know we put you in a really bad spot."

"You can make it up to us by telling us the truth," I suggested.

She took a deep breath. "Right. The truth." Rubbing the

handkerchief between her fingers, she stared down at it and started talking. "It was the police sirens that woke me up. By the time I got out of bed, the police were already at the door, talking to my parents. I didn't hear those guys break in or start beating up Neal. I wish I wasn't such a heavy sleeper. . . ."

She trailed off and stopped. Frank and I just watched her patiently, and a few seconds later she began again.

"As I walked out into the hall, Neal's door opened. He looked awful. Beat up, but more than that, more scared than I had ever seen him. Ever." She looked from Frank to me. "You guys are brothers. You know . . . when you grow up with someone, you see them at their best and their worst."

"You mean you'd seen him scared before," Frank said.

She nodded. "Right," she said. "Like, he hates roller coasters. Or you should have seen him when we rented *Paranormal Activity*. . . ." She shook her head. "Terrified. But this was way worse than that. This was like . . . he'd seen the ghost from that movie right in his bedroom. Like he'd seen the worst thing he could possibly imagine, and nothing could scare him worse."

I looked at Frank. It probably goes without saying, but that level of fear did not sound like it was caused by a football players' prank.

"I asked him what had happened," she said. "I was really worried about him. The police were there. I knew it had to be serious."

Frank nodded. "What did he say?"

She stopped and took in a breath, shaking her head. "He just said, 'Don't worry about it.'" She looked at me. "Can you believe that? Of course I was like, 'What?' and he said it again, 'Don't worry about it.'" She paused and bit her lip before continuing. "Then he took me by the shoulders," she said. "He looked me right in the eyes, and I could see how terrified he was. He said, 'Sharelle, if you care about me at all—don't worry about it. Okay?'"

I frowned. "So what did you do?" I asked.

Sharelle shrugged and looked at me again. "What could I do?" she asked. "I was really freaked out. I said okay. And then Neal said that no matter what happened, I had to back him up, and I said I would. I had never seen him like that."

I looked at Frank. I knew that he, too, was thinking about the conversation we'd just had with our dad. *Some things are best left alone.*

It seemed like Neal Bunyan certainly believed that. Even as terrible things were happening to him. What scared him—and Professor Al-Hejin, and my dad—so much? What could be worse than someone sneaking into your house in the middle of the night and beating you up?

As I was pondering this, a nurse came over. "Miss Bunyan," she said, gently touching Sharelle's shoulder, "your brother is resting in a room and ready to see you now."

Sharelle jumped up, turning back to gesture for Frank and me to follow her. "Let's go."

The nurse gently stopped her. "I'm sorry, it's immediate family only."

Sharelle stopped and regarded the nurse. She was, as I might have implied previously, not someone who was easily dissuaded. "These are my brothers," she said simply.

The nurse looked from Sharelle—who resembled a red curly-haired fireplug—to serious, dark-haired Frank, to me. I have been told I look like a young Owen Wilson without the nose. And with a chin. Which I guess means I don't look much like Owen Wilson at all. But anyway, my point: I don't look all that much like Frank, and neither one of us looks anything like Sharelle.

The nurse seemed to get this, but as quickly as she registered it, I could see that she was making a decision not to ask. "Okay," she said, and smiled sympathetically at all of us. "Please come with me."

Neal was already set up in a shared room on the third floor, but the other bed was empty. He looked bad. His right leg was in traction, he had a jagged, stitched-up cut along his right arm, and he had two black eyes. The right side of his face was all scraped up, like he'd been dragged along the street.

Looking at him, all I could think was, *Ouch.*

"Neal!" Sharelle cried, running right to his side.

Neal looked happy to see her for just a few seconds before his eyes turned to Frank and me, and his expression darkened. "What are these two doing here?"

Sharelle gave her brother a frank look. "Neal, come on. I'm not playing around anymore. You could have been killed today."

Frank stepped forward. "Look, Neal, if someone is after you, don't you think you should tell someone about it?"

Neal glared at him. "It was an accident," he said stiffly.

Sharelle looked at him in disbelief. "Are you kidding me?" she asked. "After what happened last night, you expect me to believe this was random?"

Neal looked away. "I don't care what you believe," he said. "It was an accident. Just an accident."

There was silence for a little while, and in that silence I had an idea. "Hey," I said, turning to Sharelle, "how old were you when you and Neal got into arrowheads?"

Sharelle looked at me like I was out of my mind. "What?"

Frank caught my eye and nodded. "You know," he said, stepping forward. "When you painted that little figure above Neal's bedroom door? It looked like . . ." He gestured to me. I grabbed a notepad that was on the nightstand and started drawing, pushing the pad toward Sharelle when I finished.

Her jaw dropped.

"The Red Arrow?" she asked, turning toward Neal, who was already gesturing for her to lower her voice. "You got Red Arrowed and you weren't going to tell me?"

Neal shook his head. "*Shhhh!* Keep quiet, Sharelle."

"I'm not going to keep it quiet!" Sharelle glared down at him. "You know how freaking serious this is, Neal!"

Neal sighed and looked at his sister. It was clear from his expression that he did, indeed, know how freaking serious this was.

"Um," I said, raising my hand like I was in class. "Not to interrupt, but Sharelle, could you explain to us how freaking serious this is?"

She looked at me, unamused. "Come on," she said in a low voice. "You guys have lived in Bayport your whole lives, haven't you?"

I looked at Frank, who nodded. "More or less," he agreed.

"Then how do you not know about the Red Arrow?" she asked.

I sighed. "I'm realizing that we may be the last people in town who don't know," I admitted.

"But no one will talk about it," added Frank.

Sharelle looked grim. She seemed to be gearing up to tell us what she knew, but before she could begin, Neal broke the silence.

"It's like a curse," he said weakly, staring out the window. "It's been around forever. Nobody knows where it comes from or who's behind it. But if you find the mark of the Red Arrow on your stuff, your life is basically over."

Over? I looked at Frank. "You mean, they'll kill you?"

Neal didn't respond for a moment. "No," he said finally, "or I mean, not necessarily. Maybe your business will dry up. Maybe your boss will fire you the next day. Maybe the love of your life will suddenly decide she needs to move to Reno to find herself." He stopped and looked over at us. "Maybe a couple of masked guys will break into your house and beat you up. Or maybe someone will plow into you with their car while you're crossing with the light."

I frowned, confused. "That seems like pretty serious stuff," I said. "Why not report it to the police?"

Neal scoffed. "The police!" He shook his head. "Everyone who's ever reported it to the police . . . something worse happens to them before the police can do anything."

"You mean someone on the police force is in their pocket?" Frank asked.

Neal shrugged. "Maybe." He paused. "I don't know how far up this thing goes, but nothing would surprise me. The police. Firefighters. City officials. This has gone on forever, and sometimes it stops for a few years, but it never goes away."

Hmm. I was still taking all this in. Neal was basically telling me about a criminal organization that had been operating right under our noses for our entire lives. Was it possible that the Red Arrow had always been part of Bayport, and somehow escaped Frank's and my notice?

"Neal," Sharelle said, "why do you think this is happening to you? What did you do to tick someone off?"

Neal sighed. "I don't know," he said. "I've been trying to think about it. The only possibility I can come up with is . . . Pyro Macken."

Frank raised his eyebrows at me. Pettigrew "Pyro" Macken was a notorious troublemaker, the son of a wealthy blueblood family whose father was busted years ago by our dad. Frank, in turn, busted Pett a few years ago for arson (hence the nickname "Pyro"). He was sent to juvie. Now Pett's out, and he's mostly a harmless eccentric, quarreling with his family. I don't really think he's that dangerous. But Frank thinks otherwise. "Pett Macken is a grenade with the pin pulled," he told me once. "The fuse may burn for years. But one day he's gonna go off."

"Um . . . what did you do to Pett Macken?" he asked now.

Neal sighed. He looked like he wasn't proud of what he was about to tell us. "I kind of stole his girlfriend," he said. "I mean, not really. But at this party, I met a girl he'd been seeing for a few weeks and, well, we kind of ended up kissing." He shrugged. "And then she kind of told Pyro she didn't want to see him anymore. And we dated for a few weeks."

I could see the gears turning in Frank's head. "You think he was mad enough to hurt you?" he asked. I could tell that, in Frank's estimation, it wasn't exactly outside Pett's wheelhouse to cause somebody bodily harm.

Neal looked at Frank like it was clear. "Yeah. I mean, he's kind of crazy." He stopped and fingered the long, jagged cut along his arm. Then he added, almost as an afterthought, "He really hates you two, by the way."

PETT 11

FRANK

AFTER THE WEAKLY LIT GLOOM OF THE hospital, the bright sunshine and vibrant sounds of Main Street were almost too much, too overwhelming. It seemed strange that life could go on, people could still be shopping for groceries and doing laundry and paying parking tickets, when a shadowy criminal organization was terrorizing our town.

"What do you think?" Joe asked, crossing his arms and looking up at the sky. He seemed as startled by the bright, cool day as I felt.

"I can't believe this Red Arrow thing has been going on for years and we never knew," I replied.

"I can't believe Dad knew," Joe added.

"Maybe he was protecting us," I mused, looking up and down the street. "Hey, can I say something I'm pretty sure will surprise you?"

Joe shrugged. "Sure," he said. "It seems like a day for surprises."

"I don't think Pett is behind this," I said. Joe turned to me, an eyebrow cocked. "It's too sophisticated," I went on. "Pett is a psychopath. If he was going to go after you, he would hit you over the head with something big and heavy, douse you in gasoline, and set you on fire. There'd be none of this psychological torture kind of thing."

Joe seemed to consider what I was saying. "I don't think Pett even knows the word 'psychological,'" he agreed.

"This just seems too big for him," I concluded. "Not that he couldn't be involved."

Joe sighed. "Which leaves us back at square one," he said. "If it's not Pett, who could it be?"

I sighed. It had been such a long day. I didn't have the energy to reply. And I knew I didn't need to. Joe and I know each other well enough that I knew we were both feeling the same thing.

"Hey," I said, pointing at the restaurant across the street. "Do you see that?"

"What?" Joe followed my gaze.

"Over the doorway there," I said. "Come on."

I led Joe over to the crosswalk, where we waited for the light and then crossed. (*Although that didn't help Neanderthal,*

I thought grimly.) Then we walked over to the restaurant I'd seen, which looked like it was in the process of being renovated and wasn't currently open.

Over the door, a small triangle-with-legs symbol had been painted.

"The Red Arrow," Joe and I breathed at the same time.

"So what do you think?" Joe asked. "Did the owner tick off the same person as Neanderthal?"

"Or maybe someone different, but who's involved in the same criminal organization?" I suggested. "How big do we think this thing is?"

"Neal said it was big," Joe pointed out. "Really big. Remember—he wouldn't be surprised if there were city officials involved."

I frowned, thinking that over. "Let's take a walk," I suggested.

Joe followed me as I led the way down Main Street. We took a meandering route, wandering along the side streets, through the parking lots, past city buildings.

"Look," Joe whispered, pointing at a bulkhead that led into a basement under On Second Read, the town bookstore. A tiny Red Arrow symbol had been painted there— and was already fading.

We saw another one stenciled over the window of an apartment on the second floor of a building on River Road. And a third—very tiny—painted on a bike chained to a rack in Heller Park.

"It's everywhere," I said. "Has it always been everywhere? Have we just not seen it?"

Joe shook his head but didn't reply.

"What kind of detectives are we?" I asked. "These have been hiding in plain sight for how long?"

Joe walked over to a bench and sat down. I sat down next to him. Together, we looked back at the main square of the town we'd grown up in, the town we'd almost derailed our whole future investigating and trying to clean up. Was it possible that Bayport was still keeping secrets from us?

The side door of the library opened up, and out stepped Seth Diller.

Joe groaned.

Seth didn't seem to see us as he hustled across the street and into the park. He was nearly right on top of us before his eyes narrowed in recognition and he stopped short.

"Oh," he said, not looking very psyched to see us. "Frank and Joe Hardy."

"We meet again," Joe said, nodding.

"Neal Bunyan got hit by a car," I said, not even saying hello. "We were just visiting him in the hospital."

Seth's eyes bugged out. "Are you kidding?" he asked.

I shook my head. "I wish I were," I admitted. "But it's true. It seems like someone really has it out for him."

Seth nodded slowly. It looked like there was more he wanted to say, but he didn't.

"Seth," said Joe, pulling out the sketch I had drawn in the hospital, "are you sure you can't tell us about this symbol? Neal seems to think it's related to what's happening to him."

"Really?" Seth looked surprised. But his expression quickly returned to neutral. "I don't know anything about it."

"You've never seen it before?" I pressed.

Seth looked away. "I have to go." He pushed his backpack up on his shoulder, fished some car keys out of his jeans pocket, and started walking toward the parking lot. I glanced quickly at Joe, who nodded, and we both stood up and started walking with him.

"Seth," Joe said, "man, I'm a fan of yours. We go way back. You can tell us the truth!"

"Neal told us a little bit about it," I added. "We just want to know as much as we can. We're not accusing you of anything."

Seth was speeding up. We had to work to keep up with him. We reached the parking lot, and Seth clicked the button on his keys. A *beep* sounded from a nondescript silver coupe parked near the dog run. He hustled over to it, and Joe and I followed.

About ten feet away from the car, Seth stopped short. Joe and I didn't realize at first, and we almost went plowing into him.

"Oh my—oh," Seth stammered weakly. His face was paper white.

I looked at Joe and then followed Seth's gaze to the car. Within seconds I saw what was causing Seth's distress. Something was stenciled on the driver's-side window.

The Red Arrow.

RUMORS 12

JOE

SETH TRIED TO PLAY IT COOL, LIKE HE wasn't worried, but I could see him shaking as he walked over to the driver's-side door and opened it.

"Seth, come on," I begged, moving closer. "We saw the Red Arrow. We want to help you. Let us."

He climbed into the car and put the key in the ignition.

"Seth!" I yelled, moving around and banging on the windshield. "Come on!"

Seth looked at me through the windshield, his jaw set, his expression grave. "You guys can't help me," he insisted, looking from me to Frank, who was trailing a few steps behind. "Not with this."

Without another word, Seth slammed his door and

turned the key in the ignition. I backed away from the car just in time for him to throw it in drive and peel out of the parking lot.

Frank looked as worried as I felt. "What do you think will happen to him?" he asked.

I shrugged. "Hopefully, it won't be as bad as what happened to Neanderthal," I replied. "But I'm not feeling optimistic."

Frank sighed. "Let's go home," he suggested.

Home—and a nice home-cooked meal from Aunt Trudy—sounded pretty great right now. The sun had just gone down, and the streetlights made a warm glow against the inky-blue sky. It was the kind of night that made you want to be safe at home, tucking into a bowl of spaghetti or something.

Mmmmm. Spaghetti.

That's when I heard the WEE-OO, WEE-OO of a police siren right behind us.

I turned around and groaned. A cruiser had pulled up right behind us, as quiet as a mouse. Clearly, whoever was inside was looking to startle us.

The driver opened the door and climbed out, and I can't say I was surprised.

Officer Olaf. As Neanderthal had said of Pett earlier, he really hates us. Our investigations haven't exactly made Frank and me the most popular kids in town.

What's Officer Olaf's deal? I'm not really sure. Secret

insecurity about his mustache? Not enough affection from his mother? Possibly both of those, and more. But his problem with Frank and me seems to stem from the fact that we've caught a lot of crooks in this town—a lot more than he has, frankly. And I don't think he likes that. I don't think he likes looking like the ineffective cop he is.

"Look who it is," he said now, a smile hovering insincerely below his droopy mustache, "the Hardy Boys!"

"You seem happy to see us," Frank said. He nodded politely to Olaf's rookie partner, who was sitting in the passenger seat, looking like he'd prefer to be spared this whole sordid scene.

Officer Olaf grew serious. "Happy to have found you, yes. Happy about what I have to say? No." He furrowed his bushy eyebrows. "There are rumors around town that you boys have been asking about the Red Arrow."

Gulp. Who had told Olaf? I guess it didn't matter. It's impossible to keep a secret in a town like Bayport, where everybody knows everybody else's business. You sneeze and someone three houses down says, "Bless you."

Frank shot me a surprised look, then turned to Olaf. "Huh. Who told you that?"

At this point, I was distracted. From my viewpoint I could see, behind Olaf and his cruiser, the stores of Main Street. Specifically, I had a pretty good view of the restaurant that had the Red Arrow over the doorway. As I watched, an older man with glasses, wearing a sport coat, walked up to the door, carrying a box filled with what looked like pots and kitchen stuff. He put down the box, grabbed a key from his coat pocket, and unlocked the door. Then he disappeared inside with his box.

I'm not sure why this stood out to me, but something just seemed off with this guy. I'd been curious about the owner of this restaurant and what he might have done to anger the Red Arrow. This guy didn't look like a troublemaker or anything. He looked like he might be a math teacher. Or an accountant.

"Ohhhh, I see," Frank was saying. I'd missed whatever Olaf said to explain how he'd heard about our investigations. "No, what you heard about isn't an investigation at all. Joe and I are working on a project for our civics class."

Olaf looked dubious. (To be honest, I thought it was kind of a stretch too. Frank and I aren't even in the same grade.) He leaned his elbow on the hood of the cruiser. "About the Red Arrow?" he asked. "Your teacher approved that?"

Frank didn't miss a beat. "It's taught by Coach Gerther," he said quickly.

I saw movement back on Main Street that caught my attention. Looking frustrated, the man with the glasses exited the restaurant and sighed, looking down the street, maybe toward his car. It looked like he'd forgotten something. He scurried off in that direction, not bothering to lock the door behind him.

I turned back to Olaf, who seemed to understand now.

Clearly, he was acquainted with Coach Gerther. "I see," he said. "Well, you boys know the Red Arrow is just an urban legend, don't you?" He laughed in a forced kind of way. "Do you also believe that alligators live in the sewers in New York City? Or that Pop Rocks and soda killed that kid from the Life cereal commercials?"

Frank and I started chuckling too. "Of course not," I said. "But the Red Arrow definitely has a . . . presence in this town, wouldn't you say?"

Olaf stopped laughing. "If you mean that teenagers love to whisper about the horrible things he's supposedly done, and paint that stupid symbol all over town, then sure." He stood up from the cruiser and stepped closer to us, eyes intense. I'm pretty sure he was hoping to stare us down, but that's impossible, because Olaf is a couple of inches shorter than both of us. "But let me tell you this. There's no such thing as the Red Arrow. It's just a stupid myth that encourages vandalism and distrust of the authorities. I don't want you boys legitimizing this story by asking around about it. And I especially don't want you boys investigating." He leaned even closer and dropped his voice to a whisper. "We all know what happens if you boys are caught investigating, don't we?"

I was opening my mouth to answer when it happened.

BOOOOOOOOOOOOOOOOOOOOM!

An earthshaking sound engulfed the whole center of town, so loud and startling that Frank grabbed both Olaf and me and dragged us to the ground.

Chaos erupted, people screaming and running out of buildings to see what had happened. Olaf jumped to his feet and turned to Main Street in shock.

The restaurant with the Red Arrow over the door was on fire. Well, what remained of it.

It had exploded!

A CALL FOR HELP

13

FRANK

DIDN'T SLEEP WELL THAT NIGHT DESPITE BEING exhausted, having gotten only a few hours' sleep the night before. I lay in my bed and stared at the ceiling, working the facts over and over in my mind, trying to find a way to make it all make sense.

I like for things to make sense.

An electrical fire. That was the official finding of the Bayport police and fire departments regarding the restaurant we'd watched get blown away before our very eyes. The Red Arrow stenciled above the door had been dismissed as graffiti. A teenage prank, Olaf had hissed at us, his expression practically begging us to argue with him.

Which we couldn't, of course. Joe and I were caught in a major catch-22 here. Tell the police what we knew—and why we knew it wasn't a coincidence—and we'd be admitting to doing some real investigating, therefore breaking the Deal. The J'Adoube School for Behavior Modification Therapy on Rock Island beckoned.

But that meant accepting—or pretending to accept—the Official Explanation. The restaurant's owner, a mild-mannered guy named Paul Fumusa, certainly seemed to accept it. He even admitted that he hadn't had the electrical systems inspected yet, thereby leaving him open to mishaps like this one.

But really. Let's be realistic for a second here. Bad wiring and weird electrical connections cause fires, sure.

But explosions? Big and loud enough to blow half the roof off the place, and clear the town?

Then there was the guy's face. Paul Fumusa's, I mean. His expression was a combination of shell shock and resignation that I'd seen only once before—on Neanderthal Bunyan when we showed up at his house after the beating.

Yeah. This whole scenario had Red Arrow written all over it.

Exactly what—or who—was the Red Arrow? When Joe and I had talked briefly before we hit the hay, I reminded him that when Officer Olaf scoffed at the existence of the Red Arrow, calling it an urban legend, he'd referred to the Red Arrow as "he." What if there was one person, some kind of criminal mastermind, behind the strange events of the last few days? But we'd been too exhausted to discuss this new possibility.

I sat up in bed and then climbed out, padding out of my room and down the hall to Joe's room. I pushed open his door to the sound of loud snoring.

"Seriously?" I asked, flipping on Joe's desk lamp.

Joe did not respond. He was curled up in the fetal position, hugging his comforter like a teddy bear. His mouth was open. A puddle of drool glistened on his pillow.

"JOE!" I shouted, moving closer to the bed. He jumped like he'd gotten an electrical shock. Sputtering, he looked around and spotted me sitting on the end of his bed.

"Wha?" he asked, leaning back against the headboard and wiping his mouth.

"I wanted to discuss the case," I said.

Joe stared at me, his expression going from confused to incredulous to . . . uh-oh. Kind of murderous.

I may have misjudged this one.

But luckily—I guess—for me, we were interrupted by Britney Spears.

"Hit me baby one more time!"

Joe jumped again and scrambled for his phone on his nightstand. Grabbing it, he clicked it on and held it to his ear. "Uh . . . hello?"

He scrunched up his eyebrows as he listened to whoever was on the other line. I was stumped. Who would call at this hour? Unless . . .

Joe met my eyes. "Okay," he was saying. "Okay, Seth. I know. We'll meet you at your place."

I heard squawking from the other line. Seth didn't seem to like that idea.

"Okay, okay," Joe said, nodding. "Sure. I got it. The walls have ears." He paused. "Yeah, I know where you mean. Okay. See you there in ten."

He clicked off the phone and turned to me, holding up one finger. "One," he said. *"Do not ever wake me up in the middle of the night to discuss a case."*

I was feeling a little sheepish, I must admit. "Understood," I said with a nod. "Sorry about that."

Joe nodded. "Two," he said, holding up a second finger, "we have to meet Seth Diller in the woods behind the football field. He wants to talk about the Red Arrow."

Seth had sounded totally freaked out, Joe explained as we drove through the deserted streets of Bayport for the second time in two nights. He was afraid his house was bugged, his phone was bugged. That's why he wanted to meet in person.

"Did something happen to him?" I asked, wondering what had prompted this sudden cry for help.

"I don't think so, not yet," Joe said, pulling into the parking lot behind the football field. We got out and started following a narrow path through the woods, toward a little clearing maybe half a mile in. The clearing was a popular hangout for kids to do all sorts of activities, not all of them legal. Joe and I had gotten to know it well during our investigative career.

When we reached the clearing, we saw Seth sitting on a big rock that had been covered in graffiti as long as I'd been alive. He looked nervous.

"Hey, Seth," I said, nodding in greeting. "I'm glad you called. We want to try to help you."

Seth stood. He still looked freaked. In fact, his eyes looked particularly buggy tonight. "Thanks, guys," he said. "I'm glad you showed up. I'm ready to talk about the Red Arrow."

That was weird.

"You don't have to shout it," Joe said. "The walls have ears, rememb—OOF!"

Suddenly a dark figure appeared out of the woods and tackled both Joe and me, pushing us to the ground. I wasn't able to brace myself with my hands, and I went down hard on my chest and had the wind knocked out of me. I struggled to get my bearings.

This was a setup.

I could hear the thud of fist hitting muscle as the attacker pummeled Joe, and Joe fought back. I pushed myself up and the woods spun. I could see Seth standing nervously behind our attacker, looking every bit like the weasel he was.

"This is the thanks we get for trying to help you?" I managed, still struggling to get my breath.

But then I heard a buzzing sound and looked over at my brother and the attacker. He was wearing a David Letterman mask. And he had a Taser!

"No!" I shouted as I leaped forward, grabbing the thing out of his hand right before he applied the electrical current to my still-struggling brother. That got the attacker's attention. He immediately turned to me, lunging to get the Taser back, but he only succeeded in knocking it out of my hand. He threw his whole weight on me, pinning me to the ground. I used all my best self-defense training (Dad insisted, back in the day) to get free, but this guy was all arms. I placed a few well-aimed punches, but at my odd angle, I was able to land only a few.

I could tell the guy was tiring out, though. Maybe whoever had sent him hadn't mentioned that there would be two victims. He crawled forward, and I could tell he was going for the Taser.

But then Joe suddenly stood up behind him, the Taser in his right hand! He was panting, still trying to catch his breath from his own struggle with this guy.

Joe pressed the sides of the Taser, and the electrical current sizzled, bright blue-white.

"You want to tell us what the heck's going on?" he asked. "Or would you like to meet my friend Mr. Sparky?"

MISCHIEF 14

JOE

I DO NOT LIKE GETTING WOKEN UP. I MEAN, REALLY.

Aunt Trudy used to wake us for school in the mornings, but after a few well-aimed pillows to her head, she bought me an *extremely loud* alarm clock and said I was on my own.

So when I was woken from a sound sleep for the second night in a row—by Frank, technically, and I had not forgotten that, but really by that weasel Seth Diller—I was getting answers.

The Taser felt almost too good in my hands.

"Did you hear me?" I demanded, holding the Taser closer to our attacker and letting the current crackle. He shrank back.

I turned around and held the Taser out to Seth. I hadn't

forgotten he was back there. "Or you?" I demanded. "You seem depressed, Seth. Maybe some nice electroshock therapy would help?"

"Hey, hey, hey." Frank suddenly stood beside me and gently—very gently—reached out to take the Taser. "Why don't we all just calm down? Nice and calm. Totally non-electrically calm." He held out his hand, and reluctantly, I dropped the Taser into it.

"I want answers," I whispered to my brother.

"Let's not get arrested," he hissed back.

Seth and Dave (Letterman) still looked pretty freaked, though. Seth's eyes were the buggiest I'd ever seen them. And Dave was shaking.

"Take off the mask," I ordered Dave, hoping that just knowing we had the Taser now would be enough.

It was, apparently. The attacker reached up and pushed the mask back over his head.

I saw his face and gasped.

Pett Macken!

"Neanderthal was right!" I cried. "This wasn't too sophisticated for you after all!"

Pett's dull eyes drilled into mine, mystified. "Sophisticated?" he asked.

Frank held out his hand. "Slow down, slow down," he said, stepping forward and gesturing for Pett and Seth to sit down. "Why don't you two tell us what happened—in your own words?"

The two boys sat, Seth sighing deeply.

"I don't know exactly what happened," he said, running a hand over his face.

"Tell us what you know," I urged.

"Okay." Seth looked at the ground. "I saw the Red Arrow on my car this evening, when you guys were there. You saw it with me."

Frank nodded. "Why do you think you were targeted?"

Seth shrugged. "I'm not sure," he said. "Really. My best guess, though, is that I'm being punished for talking about it with you two."

That had me pretty skeptical. "Talking about it with us? How would anybody know?"

Seth glared at me. "You really are naive, aren't you?" he asked. "It's like I told you just now. The walls have ears. I'm sure somebody is listening to this conversation as we speak."

I'm not proud of this, but those words sent a little chill down my spine.

"Okay," said Frank. "So you see that you're targeted. What then? How did we get here?"

Seth looked down at his hands. "I was woken up in the middle of the night by a phone call," he replied.

"Sounds familiar," I said. "And?"

Seth shivered. "It was this creepy voice," he replied. "Distorted, like someone talking through a pipe. It was from a number I'd never seen before. The voice told me that if I did something for him—if I helped him get you two—he'd let me off. The Mark of the Red Arrow would be lifted."

I glanced at my brother. So the Red Arrow knew about us. They—or he—knew enough to want to stop us.

That wasn't good.

I turned to Pett, who was sitting there like a bump on a log (literally). "What about you?"

Pett looked up, like he'd just remembered he was part of this conversation. "What about me?"

"How did you get involved with the Red Arrow, Pett?" Frank spelled out slowly.

Pett shook his head. "I don't know," he said. "I don't know what I did to make him mad. I came home one day, and there was a mark on my motorcycle."

"You have no idea what you did to prompt it?" I asked.

Pett shook his head.

"Pett probably does all kinds of despicable things every day," Frank said quietly to me.

I sighed. Man, I was tired. "Okay, okay. You don't know why you got Red Arrowed. But how did you get here?"

Pett looked confused. "I rode my bike?"

Frank groaned. "Why did you beat us up, Pett?"

"Oh!" Pett, seeming to grasp his place in this investigation at last, sat straighter on the log. "Well, a couple of months ago, I got a call like Seth here," he said, gesturing to Seth. Seth shrank back, like he didn't want to be associated.

"Same distorted voice?" Frank asked. "Same unfamiliar number?"

Pett nodded. "The voice told me that I could avoid any further punishment—that's what it said—by doing some jobs for him." He paused. "Or her. It could be a her, I guess."

"Odd jobs?" I asked. "Like pummeling people?"

Pett nodded again. "I beat some people up, sure," he said. He held up his left arm and flexed it. "I guess I'm lucky I've got some muscle."

Frank caught my eye. I could tell he was disgusted. "And that's why you came here tonight?" he said.

"That's right," said Pett. "I got a call telling me I had another odd job. And then it turned out to be you guys." He grinned.

"That was lucky," I said, trying to interpret the grin.

"Sure," said Pett. "It was a job I enjoyed, after what you boys did to me."

Frank held up the Taser and sparked it, once. "Didn't exactly turn out great for you," he pointed out.

Pett just glared at him, then looked away.

I closed my eyes for a moment. "All right," I said, holding up my hands. "I think we're done for the night, gentlemen. Let's all go home and get some sleep."

Seth looked surprised. "That's it?" he asked.

I was about to say yes—or *We'll talk about it in the morning*—when I was interrupted by the blaring of a police siren.

Seth's eyes widened. "Uh-oh."

It was coming from the parking lot. I looked at Frank.

"Uh-oh," he whispered.

Before we could move, I heard footsteps running down the path.

"Freeze!" Olaf's voice came through the trees before he even surfaced at the path's end.

I looked at Frank and slowly held up my hands. He followed suit. No need to anger Olaf in the wee hours of the morning, I figured.

Again. We were having a really banner week.

Olaf appeared at the end of the path, his rookie partner behind him. Both were brandishing weapons.

"Hands up!" Olaf yelled. Frank and I were way ahead of him, but Seth and Pett slowly followed suit.

Olaf moved in and slowly circled the four of us, casing the location. "Okay," he said after a few seconds. "I'm going to march you all back to the cruiser, and you're coming back to the station with me. Understand?"

"What?" Pett asked in a surly tone. "Why? For what?"

Olaf glared at him. "Oh, it's you," he said snootily. "Back to jail so soon? We've received noise complaints about a fight going on out here." He paused and looked me right in the eye. "We're taking you all in for criminal mischief."

Criminal mischief. A charge that can conveniently encompass basically any reason a cop might take a dislike to you. Frank and I had been brought in for criminal mischief before. Most likely, we'd be brought in again . . . and again. And again.

That didn't mean our parents liked it much, of course.

As we all marched behind Olaf and his partner back to the cruiser, I caught Frank's eye again. He cocked an eyebrow. "Does this seem like a place with a lot of neighbors to you?" he whispered.

He was right. The reason kids could get away with all kinds of various activities in these woods was that they were completely secluded . . . from everything. The nearest houses were at least a half mile away. Too far to hear the fight we'd had.

So what was really going on here?

A TIP 15

FRANK

WAS STARTING TO GET RED ARROW VISION.
Everyone who appeared in front of me, I imagined as the
Red Arrow. Officer Olaf. Chief Gomez. Even Hattie,
the kindly longtime receptionist at the Bayport Police
Department.

Clearly, I was losing it.

Joe and I were almost immediately ushered into Chief
Gomez's office as Pett and Seth were led into a different room.

He didn't exactly look thrilled to see us. But then, we
rarely met on happy occasions.

"Boys," he said, inclining his head and looking from Joe
to me.

"Chief Gomez," Joe said, "this is all a big misunderstanding."

Gomez laughed. "Oh, sure. I've never heard that from you boys before."

"It's true," I threw in. I didn't actually expect him to believe me, but it was worth a shot. "We were just having a conversation with Pett and Seth when Officer Olaf showed up."

Gomez rolled his eyes at me. "Just a conversation," he said, deadpan. "At three o'clock in the morning. In a deserted part of town."

"That reminds me," Joe piped up, sitting a little straighter in his chair. "Who called in the noise complaint? There aren't any houses anywhere near those woods."

Chief Gomez's expression turned hard, like he was tired of humoring us. "That's classified information." He leaned forward. "Listen, boys, I thought we had a deal." He lowered his voice. "The Deal. Sound familiar?"

I looked at Joe. Time to get serious. "Of course it does, sir," I said, putting on my best altar-boy face.

Gomez sighed, like he was just as tired as we were. "I've been hearing rumors that you boys are doing some investigative work around town," he said. "That would be unfortunate, wouldn't it? After we worked so hard to get the Deal in place."

Joe leaned forward. "We haven't been investigating, sir," he said, "but we have been asking a few questions about the Red Arrow."

Gomez looked at him. "The Red Arrow," he repeated, no emotion in his voice.

"It's a symbol we've seen a lot around town," I said. "Some

people seem to think it's related to a . . . a curse, of sorts."

Gomez looked at me hard, then cleared his throat. "Listen, boys," he said, "I'm not thrilled about the Deal either. I want you boys to be safe, but you've contributed a lot to the town over the years, and I . . . well, I'll admit it. Sometimes I miss your input on a case here or there." He paused. "But I certainly don't enjoy hearing that you boys are jeopardizing your future over some urban legend. Some ghost story teenagers tell each other at slumber parties."

Joe shot me a nervous glance. "But what if . . . what if, without investigating, Frank and I stumbled on some information implying that the Red Arrow is very real?"

Chief Gomez looked from Joe to me, shaking his head. "I'd say great," he said, lowering his voice and moving closer. "Care to tell me what it is? And how you got it?"

I looked at Joe, subtly swiping my hand across my neck. Cut it out. Catch-22. "No, sir," I said.

"Listen." Gomez smacked his meaty hand on the top of his desk. "I want this to end. I don't want to be called into the station at three a.m. to give you this warning again." He gave us another serious look. "Stop sniffing around. Follow the Deal. Don't put your whole future in jeopardy."

Just then the phone on his desk rang. The chief frowned at us as if to say *Quiet!* And then picked it up.

"Yes? . . . Okay. Okay. Yes, understood."

He hung up the phone and gave us an insincere smile. "Boys, after consulting with your father, we have decided to drop all charges against you." He leaned forward. "But you'd better stay out of trouble from now on. Understand?"

"Absolutely, sir," I said, standing up. Phew! Fenton Hardy comes through again.

Chief Gomez led us out of his office, grabbing his jacket on the way out. "I'm going home to get some sleep," he told us.

Sleep. Much as I'd struggled with it earlier that night, it sounded divine. Gomez led us out to the lobby, where Hattie informed us that our aunt Trudy was on her way. I glanced at Joe, wondering if that was a bad omen.

"Is Dad going to kill us?" I whispered, taking a seat on an uncomfortable chair.

Joe shrugged. "I think we have a fifty-fifty shot," he replied.

I'm not sure how long it was before Aunt Trudy showed up. Truth be told, I may have dozed a bit. Joe too. Joe did ask about Pett and Seth, and was told they'd been released about half an hour before us.

Before I knew it, Hattie was calling, "Boys?" and Joe and I startled awake. Aunt Trudy was standing before us, smiling tensely.

"Hi, Aunt Trudy," Joe said. "We really appreciate you picking us up. Are Mom and Dad, um . . . ?"

"Apoplectic?" Aunt Trudy supplied, her smile warming. "You'll have to ask them. Your dad came up to wake me and ask me to come get you, then holed himself up in his study. I didn't get much besides 'boys' and 'police station.'

And 'again.'" You mother went to bed early not feeling well, and doesn't know yet."

I looked at Joe. "Uh-oh."

He nodded. "That doesn't sound good."

I stood up and chatted with Aunt Trudy about her garden while Hattie passed our belongings back to us, and Joe ran to use the men's room. When he came back, he grabbed my arm. "Maybe you should use the restroom too before we leave," he said, giving me a meaningful look.

I looked at Aunt Trudy. "That's not a bad idea," I said.

She waved her hand. "Sure, sure, go ahead. It's not like my bed is calling for me or anything."

Joe gave her a smile. "We owe you big-time, Aunt Trudy. What if Frank and I cook dinner tonight?"

Aunt Trudy grimaced. "Ugh. What have I done to earn such punishment?" she asked.

Joe shrugged. "Well, we'll figure out something. I'm, ah, going to grab a drink from the water fountain."

He followed me back down the hall to the restrooms, then grabbed my arm again. "Check it out."

He was holding out his wallet, billfold open to reveal a note written in thick black marker on yellow lined paper.

CHECK OUT THE RESTAURANT.

"It was in my wallet when I picked it up," Joe whispered.

I looked at him incredulously. "It had to have been left

by someone in the police department," I whispered back to him.

Joe nodded. "Or someone who was arrested, maybe."

I shook my head. "They wouldn't have access to people's belongings."

"Either way," Joe said, "we need to get over there. We'll need something to distract Aunt Trudy."

I nodded. "On it," I said. "Operation Trudy Distraction, in full effect!"

"Ouch!" I cried as I fake-stumbled down the last step from police headquarters to Main Street. "Oh, ow! Man! Hold on, you guys. My ankle."

Joe and Aunt Trudy turned around, Aunt Trudy looking concerned, Joe impressed.

"What happened, Frank?" Aunt Trudy asked.

I made a big show of hopping around, like my ankle was injured. "I think I twisted it," I said, then sighed. "Oh, man! It's going to be a struggle to get down the steps to the parking lot."

Aunt Trudy looked grim. "Do we need to take you to the hospital? Do you need an X-ray?"

"No!" I cried, and noticed that Joe seemed to just stop himself in time from shouting it with me.

"I'll just put some ice on it when we get home," I added. "This happens to me a lot. I must have weak ankles."

Aunt Trudy pursed her lips. "Well, if you say so. I

suppose I'll need to get the car and bring it around for you."

I nodded. "That would be great, Aunt Trudy. Thanks."

Aunt Trudy turned to Joe. He seemed to realize after a few seconds that she was waiting for him to go with her.

I moved closer to Joe and leaned on his shoulder. "It would be great if Joe could stay with me," I said. "To lean on."

Aunt Trudy shrugged. "Well, I guess so," she said. "I'll be right around with the car. You boys stay put."

We waited until she was halfway down the stairs to the parking lot, then dashed down the street to the remains of Paul Fumusa's restaurant.

The blown-out windows had been masked with plastic, and scorch marks covered the exterior. It was pitch-dark inside, but the Hardy Boys come prepared. I pulled out a key chain with a super-bright flashlight on the end and shone it into the restaurant.

We could make out charred remains of tables and chairs. Debris. What looked like a burned umbrella handle.

But nothing that meant anything to us. Nothing we could point to and say, *Here's the key to the secret identity of the Red Arrow!*

Which is sort of what I'd been hoping for, I admit.

"Do you get it?" Joe asked, watching me aim the flashlight back and forth.

"No," I admitted with a sigh. I had no idea what was going on here.

Beep, beep! We both turned around to see Aunt Trudy in her little hybrid, looking surprised—and annoyed—to see me walking just fine.

We ran over to her and jumped into the car.

"I bent my ankle this one way and then totally recovered," I said, feeling my cheeks burn at the lie. "It's a miracle!"

WATCHED 16

JOE

IT WAS CLEAR, BY THE TIME WE GOT HOME, THAT it was going to take a lot more than dinner to get back on Aunt Trudy's good side.

"You'd better go in and talk to your father," she huffed as she got out of the car and slammed the door.

They were the first words she'd spoken since Frank had told her about his miracle recovery.

I looked at my brother, and we both sighed. What a long, miserable night. Upsetting our beloved aunt Trudy was just the icing on the cake.

But there was still more to come. We had to talk to Dad.

We went into the house and slowly approached his study, then knocked quietly.

"Dad?" I called.

"Come in," he replied in a gruff voice. I looked at my brother.

"Here goes," I whispered, and pushed the door open.

"Dad," Frank said before we even crossed the threshold, "we can explain."

"Can you?" asked Dad, standing up and walking around the desk. "Can you? Really?"

Without another word, he brushed by us and out of his study. We had no choice but to follow him down the hallway, through the foyer and to the front door, which he opened.

"There," he said, stepping out and pointing up over the doorway.

I had a sickening realization before I looked. It couldn't be. But of course it was. It only made sense. . . .

There, stenciled above our front door, was the Red Arrow.

"Dad," I managed. But no more words would come.

He looked hard at me, then Frank. "Let's go back to my study."

We followed him back through the door, the foyer, the hall, to his study. He closed the door behind us, and Frank and I dropped exhaustedly into the chairs facing his desk. Dad picked up a mug of probably cold coffee and took a swig. (He still drinks it long after it's gone cold. Frank calls this "gross." I call it "hard-core.")

When he'd finished, he put the coffee cup down and sat

down behind his desk, looking at both of us through hooded eyes. Dad looked as tired as I felt.

"I thought," he said after a few uncomfortable moments, "we had an agreement."

I took a deep breath.

"We did, Dad," Frank said, sitting forward in his chair. "But look, Joe and I believe—you taught us—that if something wrong is happening in this town, and people are getting hurt, then we should do everything within our power to fix it."

Dad stared at him. "Really? Up to and including putting your own family in jeopardy?"

Frank shook his head. "We didn't mean to do that."

"I thought I was very clear the last time we talked," Dad went on, his voice low. "Some things are better left alone. And you didn't leave this alone."

Neither one of us answered. Our father eyeballed us for a moment more, then dropped his gaze to the desk.

"It makes me wonder," he went on, "how much I can trust you two in general anymore. For example, keeping up the Deal." He looked up at us.

Frank and I didn't say anything. It was sort of an unspoken agreement between us that he, Dad, and I never mentioned the Deal. Honestly, it hurt too much. I don't think any of us liked to be reminded of what we had lost in the Deal—or at least, lost the right to do openly.

But at the same time, the Deal was the only thing securing

us a decent future. College and a job and a family and kids one day. Without the Deal, it was the J'Adoube School for Behavior Modification Therapy on Rock Island. Which was not the kind of future anybody wanted.

For a few minutes, nobody spoke.

Finally Dad leaned across his desk. "As I have told you," he said, "there are powerful forces at work here. I really don't think you boys know what you're getting into. If you care about me, if you care about your own future, please just leave well enough alone."

"But, Dad," Frank said, "how do you know? Were you Red Arrowed before?"

Dad was quiet for a few seconds. "No," he said. "I was never that unlucky. But I've had clients who were."

I looked at Frank. There was a question forming on my tongue, but I was almost afraid to ask it.

Fortunately, my brother and I think alike—and he is sometimes braver than I am. "What happened to them?" he asked.

But my father never got the chance to reply.

He was cut off by a bloodcurdling scream from upstairs. Aunt Trudy!

Aunt Trudy stood in my room, my backpack dropped before her on the floor.

"It's watching me," she whispered when the three of us appeared. "It's watching. . . ."

"What's going on?" My parents' bedroom door opened and out stumbled my mother, hair tousled, wearing her signature satin pajamas. She looked from Dad to me to Frank to Aunt Trudy. "Who was that screaming? What are you all doing up?"

Dad turned to look from Mom to Aunt Trudy. "It was Trudy screaming," he said. "It's a long story. But, Trudy—who's watching? What do you mean?"

Aunt Trudy backed out of my bedroom, pointing at a plastic robot on my bookshelf. I built it in the second grade. His name is Mike the Robot.

But behind Mike the robot . . .

A red light blinked. And a lens pointed.

Watching.

Waiting.

"We're being videotaped!" Aunt Trudy cried.

THE JOY OF PUBLIC SPEAKING

17

FRANK

I**T'S A PRETTY HUGE KICK IN THE PANTS TO** have to go to school on the day after two sleepless nights, after being beaten up, arrested, chewed out by your father, marked for punishment by the mastermind of a shady criminal organization, and monitored in your own home.

It's an even bigger kick in the pants to have to go to school on the day after two sleepless nights, after being beaten up, arrested, chewed out by your father, marked for punishment by the mastermind of a shady criminal organization, and monitored in your own home . . . only to have to give a speech on civil liberties that you have not prepared for in any way!

That's right. I, Frank Hardy, Extreme Public Speaking Fraidy-Pants and Meticulous Student Extraordinaire, was now facing my worst nightmare: giving a speech. In front of more than three hundred students. Did I mention I hate public speaking?

"Maybe you can tell Ms. Jones the truth and ask for more time," Joe suggested as we pulled into the school parking lot.

Yes. That had every chance in the world of working, with the week I'd been having.

"Which version of the truth?" I asked. "The one where I was distracted by the shady criminal organization no one will admit exists in this town?"

Joe nodded, his face grim. "Yeah. Better to just fake your way through it, I guess."

Oh, to be my brother sometimes. To be a person for whom "just faking your way through" a speech in front of three hundred people is an option. I sometimes wonder what happened with Joe and me where he got the exact opposite genes that I did. I mean, except for the sleuthing gene.

And admittedly, we both have pretty good hair.

We'd managed to disable the video camera we'd found last night, but we were still very aware of the Red Arrow mark on our heads, so we tried to lie low all morning. We didn't really expect that anyone would try anything during school hours, but really, who knew?

"Ready for your speech?" Ms. Jones asked with a big smile when I walked into American history class third period.

"I'm a little nervous," I admitted.

"Oh, you'll be fine." She gave me a little pat on the shoulder, then paused. "You're not . . . going to say anything unusual, are you?"

Unusual? What did that mean?

"I have a section written in Martian," I replied with a smile. "Is that too weird?"

Ms. Jones looked confused for a moment, then chuckled. "Oh, Frank," she said. "I'm sure you'll be fine."

Funny how everybody who was not me was so sure of that.

My speech was to take place at 11:20 sharp—fourth period. I tried to lose myself in Ms. Jones's lecture about trench fighting during World War I, but I couldn't concentrate. Later, when I looked back at my notes, I found a sketch of a noose with *HELP ME* written all around it.

I had to ask for a bathroom pass four times in forty-five minutes.

Then, all too soon, the bell rang.

Ms. Jones smiled at me like I'd just won the lottery. "Well, class," she said, "let's make our way to the auditorium, where we'll hear your classmate Frank Hardy's brilliant presentation on civil liberties!"

There were some cheers, some groans. A football player exercised his civil liberties by throwing an eraser at my head when Ms. Jones walked out the door. "Brownnoser," he hissed.

Oh, if only those were my only problems. If only I'd be crying myself to sleep that night because the football players didn't like me, and not because I'd wet myself in front of three hundred people.

I followed Ms. Jones to the auditorium like a dead man walking. People talked to me, greeting me, I guess, or wishing me luck, but I didn't hear any of it. Keeping up a steady stream of pep talk, Ms. Jones led me around the gym to the backstage entrance to the auditorium, which would lead me onto the stage.

She opened the door, and I could hear the dull roar of my three-hundred-some classmates, none of them (except for Joe, of course) prepared for the meltdown they were about to witness.

I tried not to look out into the audience. Ms. Jones walked up to the podium, which had been set in the middle of the stage, to introduce me, talking about why she had chosen my "exceptional" paper to be presented to the entire school. It was something about the importance of preserving our civil liberties, even in this day and age, blah, blah, blah. I couldn't make out much beyond the sound of blood pounding in my head.

But I could tell she was winding down.

"And without further ado," Ms. Jones went on, "let me present to you . . . your classmate, Frank Hardy!"

There were a couple of random boos—to be expected, really—but mostly polite applause. I forced my feet to move one after the other and carry me onstage. The applause intensified. I managed to smile at Ms. Jones and make it to the podium without passing out.

I looked out at the packed auditorium. Hundreds of faces stared back at me. I tried to locate Joe in the crowd, but it was impossible. My breathing sped up, and I remembered the top piece of advice Joe had given me: Imagine everyone in the audience in their underwear.

It didn't help much.

I touched the microphone, tapping it gently to make sure it was on, and then pulled it close to my mouth.

A deep, shuddery breath reverberated throughout the auditorium.

"Civil liberties," I forced myself to say, smoothing the paper with my notes out in front of me, "are a crucial element of our democracy."

Creeeeaaaak.

The heavy double doors at the rear of the auditorium slowly opened, and light from the lobby flooded in behind a dark silhouette, which leaned on a cane. The silhouette moved forward, and the lights of the auditorium illuminated Principal Gorse. He noted that I was staring at him and nodded encouragingly in my direction. His kind brown eyes crinkled at the corners. He stepped forward, slowly, and the bright lights flashed off the cane in his hand. It was shiny silver metal; it looked like something NASA might have designed. Totally different from his old hand-carved cane. When had he gotten it?

Someone in the audience coughed, "Narc," and I startled back to attention. ("Narc" is the affectionate nickname bestowed on Joe and myself by some of our classmates—mostly, the friends of people we've busted.) I realized I'd been silent for about thirty seconds and smoothed my paper again. Sheesh, my hands were sweaty.

"Civil liberties," I said loudly, "are . . ."

And then, suddenly, it hit me like a bolt of lightning.

The note that had been slipped into Joe's wallet: *CHECK OUT THE RESTAURANT*. And the charred umbrella handle.

It hadn't been an umbrella handle. It had been a cane.

Principal Gorse's cane!

I hated the thought that our kindly principal might be behind the terrible things the Red Arrow had done, but the more I thought about it, the more sense it made. Neal, Seth, and Pett had all brought shame to Principal Gorse—in some small way—by being busted for a crime while attending Bayport High School. I had no idea what Paul Fumusa had done to him, but surely there was more to Principal Gorse's life than the little bit we saw at school. Maybe Paul Fumusa had flirted with Ms. Collins or rear-ended the Karmann Ghia or told Principal Gorse that turtlenecks with sport coats were over.

I was paralyzed, standing there.

"Narc says what?" someone finally hissed from the second row.

It was enough to shake me out of my thoughts.

"Civil liberties," I began, "are . . ."

A farce in this town, I thought.

131

I put my elbows on the podium and leaned on them, suddenly feeling . . . angry.

"You know what?" I barked suddenly into the mic, startling the people sitting closest. "This whole speech is all kinds of bull, because the biggest threat to our civil liberties in the town of Bayport is the one no one will talk about." I leaned right into the mic, enjoying the feeling of the words slipping out of my mouth. "The Red Arrow."

I could see people in the audience looking shocked, sitting a little straighter, a *Did I just hear that?* expression on their faces. That's when I spotted Joe. He was sitting on the aisle, about midway back, and his jaw was hanging open.

"There, I said it," I went on. "Is everyone scared? Is lightning going to strike me from above? Because that's how he keeps his power, you know. No one will talk about it. No one will talk about what the Red Arrow is doing."

People were squirming now. I looked back at Principal Gorse, and his face wore an expression I'd never seen on him before: pure rage. He was turning scarlet, his eyebrows drawing harsh lines over his eyes, which bugged in horror.

He began marching down the aisle—as fast as he could manage with the space-age cane.

"So let's talk about what he's doing," I went on. "He's beating kids up. Forcing them to do his bidding. Even spying on their cell phone conversations."

Principal Gorse reached the foot of the stage and began

struggling up the three stairs. Having no idea why he was climbing up, I'm sure, Ms. Jones rushed forward to give him a hand.

"Who knows how far up his influence goes?" I asked. "Is the Red Arrow connected with the police? With town officials? Even . . . school officials?"

Principal Gorse lurched up the last step and immediately lunged in my direction. I actually had to swerve away to avoid being tackled by the man. He looked like a hungry wolf, like he would have happily chewed me up and spit me out right there if he could.

Instead he grabbed the mic. "This speech is over," he panted. "I need to meet with Frank . . . immediately."

The din in the auditorium immediately rose to study-hall levels, all the students wanting to know what was happening, what I had done. Ms. Jones ran over, brows furrowed in confusion.

"Simon?" she asked, touching Principal Gorse's shoulder. "What's . . . happening? Are you . . . ?"

Joe, who'd jumped up in his seat the minute Principal Gorse took the mic, ran up the aisle and onto the stage. "I'll go too!" he blurted, running to my side. "I . . . I . . ."

"I suppose we all have a lot to talk about," I said, giving Principal Gorse a meaningful look.

He nodded. "Come with me," he said, moving off toward the wings of the stage.

With Ms. Jones still mystified, and the teachers in the

audience struggling to regain control of their students as chaos broke out, Joe and I followed Principal Gorse through the wings and out a door that led to a quiet hallway behind the gym.

When he turned to face us, Principal Gorse's face was completely different. The rage was gone. In its place I thought I saw regret.

"Okay," he said, his voice low as his eyes darted around the hallway. "Clearly, you boys are in need of . . . answers. Answers I think I can provide."

I nodded. "Go on."

He took a breath and stopped. "I would like to do this somewhere private," he went on. "I promise, when I finish what I have to say, I will leave myself at your mercy. Looking back, I see where I have gone wrong. I know that I must be punished. Understand?"

Joe looked from the principal to me, and I could tell he was mystified but going to play along. He nodded.

I nodded too, turning back to the man I believed to be the Red Arrow. "Principal Gorse, you know we've always respected you. I don't want to make this more difficult than it needs to be." I paused. "But I think I need to call the police now. I hope you understand."

I pulled out my phone and started dialing the Bayport PD's number. Before I could get past the first digit, Principal Gorse silently put his hand on my phone and stopped me.

"Do you want to know the truth or not?" he asked evenly.

I looked at Joe. He looked as surprised as I felt. Of course we wanted to know the truth. But I wanted to be safe, too.

The principal lowered his voice. "Come with me," he said, "and I'll tell you everything. Call the police now, and I'll cooperate, yes—but I won't answer their questions. I won't give you any of the answers you want."

Joe widened his eyes at me. I didn't know what to do. I knew we shouldn't trust Gorse . . . but I needed to know what the Red Arrow really was. Why such a seemingly nice man had done this.

Principal Gorse eyed me sympathetically. "You may keep your cell phone on, of course," he said. "If you feel uncomfortable at any time, the police are just three digits away, no?"

I swallowed and looked at Joe. It sounded reasonable. Maybe we weren't going to get to the bottom of the Red Arrow without taking a risk.

"Okay," I said finally.

Gorse gave an abrupt nod. "I appreciate that, boys. If you'll follow me . . . I know a place where we can talk privately."

He took out a key and led us through a small doorway and down a flight of steps. We were entering the fabled Bayport High School basement. Depending on who you talked to, the bodies of failing seniors were buried down there, or the secret room where teachers kept all the answer keys, or a forgotten dungeon. Unlike the Red Arrow, though, those were actual urban legends.

Principal Gorse paused before a metal door and then pushed it open. Blinding sunlight streamed in. We walked out onto the football field.

To the right was an area that had been under construction for the past few months. Rumor had it that we were getting a new gym and locker rooms, but right now the place just looked like a mud farm with some construction equipment and storage containers. Principal Gorse approached one of these containers and pulled out a key.

"This has been my secret office for some time," he said quietly. "I've come out here whenever I was doing something I didn't wish for anyone to witness. I keep a laptop in here and make all my phone calls on a disposable cell phone."

How long had this been going on? I wondered. Had Principal Gorse always been the Red Arrow, even when our dad was struggling with it? I hoped we'd get the truth once we stepped inside.

The principal unlocked the heavy padlock, pushed the heavy metal door open, and walked inside. The room was narrow, rectangular, and dim, with a tiny bit of light filtering in from a hatch in the ceiling that was open just a crack.

I looked back at Joe and followed Principal Gorse inside. Joe was close behind. We stood in the room, blinking as our eyes slowly adjusted.

The room was cold, and totally empty. Then I spotted

something strange. The end of a hose had been fed through the narrow opening of the hatch. At that moment, Principal Gorse suddenly lunged at me, swinging his cane at my head.

"AAUUUGH!" I ducked just in time, but the tip of the cane cracked Joe, who'd been rushing to my defense, in the nose. Blood spurted in all directions.

"What the—?" I managed, as Principal Gorse brought the cane back and swung it again.

I careened to the side, but it still hit me flush in the shoulder, knocking me to the ground and making me moan with pain.

Principal Gorse aimed a quick, nasty kick at Joe's leg and sent him tumbling to the ground too. He stood over us, brandishing the cane like a baseball bat.

"You idiot Hardys," he hissed in a gravelly voice I'd never heard before. Did our principal have multiple personalities? Or was this all a sleep-deprivation-induced hallucination?

No. He stumbled over to the door, kneeling down to turn something just out of sight. Immediately I heard water trickling into the hose. Within a few seconds, a steady gush poured out of the hose into the container.

"This storage container is completely watertight," Principal Gorse went on.

He grabbed two chairs, then pulled us up roughly, slamming us into our seats, and started tying us up with rope that was lying nearby. "You'll note there's no drain in the room.

No, this container is going to fill up slowly, leaving you boys plenty of time to ponder your last breath and how you got to this point."

I was able to reach into my pocket for my cell phone and quickly dialed 911.

Nothing happened.

I looked at the screen. No!

NO SIGNAL.

Principal Gorse chuckled. "I've made note of the various places around the school where cellular service drops out," he said. "There are so many of them! It's almost as though someone was tampering with the signal."

He walked through the door, grabbing the edge to slam it.

I tried to lunge to my feet, but I couldn't really move, thanks to the pain and the rope. Gorse let out an eerie laugh as the metal door shut behind him. I heard him replacing the padlock on the chain, leaving Joe and me trapped inside.

GUSH 18

JOE

'D NEVER REALLY HAD A FEAR OF DROWNING until that door clanked shut behind Principal Gorse. It's a pretty terrible way to die, when you think about it. First off, you have plenty of time to realize that you're dying. Plus, from what I have gathered, slowly running out of air is not really a comfortable way to go.

"How do we get out of here?" I asked Frank, struggling against the rope. Already the floor was nearly covered by a growing puddle. The water was coming in fast.

Frank groaned. He wriggled around and managed to work his way out. "That cane felt like a baseball bat," he muttered, making his way over to me.

"Maybe that's why he got the metal upgrade," I suggested. Frank worked at the rope and got me free. I winced as I stood up, rubbing my shoulder. I paused. "For real, Frank, how did you figure out that Principal Gorse is the Red Arrow?"

"It was the cane." Frank stood with a groan. "I remembered the debris we saw in the restaurant. There was something that looked like an umbrella handle—remember?"

Riiiiight. "Yeah. When we got that note we couldn't figure out."

"It wasn't an umbrella handle," Frank went on. "It was a cane. Principal Gorse's old cane."

Aha. "And Neal, Seth, Pett—they all got in trouble while at Bayport High."

"Maybe they disgraced him in some way. I don't know," Frank said. "And I haven't figured out how Paul Fumusa plays into it. But clearly, Principal Gorse has been hiding a lot from us."

He stopped and looked around the room. "Do you see anything we could use to stand on to reach the hose?"

I looked around. The room was really dark, lit only by the light seeping in from the opening around the hatch. "Not really," I admitted. "This thing is pretty tall."

The water was deepening, up to our ankles now. The stream from the hose splashed into the pool. My feet were soaked, and it was getting harder to walk around.

"Hey, Frank," I said.

He turned around, curious.

"That was a great speech."

He let out a short laugh and shook his head. "I hope it doesn't turn out to be my swan song."

I could tell he was getting nervous. Truthfully, I was too. We'd gone up against a lot of nasty characters before. But the Red Arrow had been operating in Bayport and avoiding detection for years. Even Fenton Hardy feared him. Was he smart enough to defeat us? Had the Hardy Boys met their match?

That's when I heard banging on the door.

"What the . . . ?" Frank muttered.

I sloshed over to the metal door. "Hello?" I yelled.

I could barely make out the voice on the other side over the rushing water.

"Frank? Joe? Is that you?"

The voice was nasally. Female. I looked at my brother.

Sharelle!

"Sharelle, are you out there?" I shouted. "Please help us! Can you open the door?"

I heard grunting and clanking as Sharelle yanked on the chain. "It won't budge!"

"Gorse has the key!" I cried.

"I knew you were acting weird during your speech, Frank," Sharelle called. "I snuck away from my class and followed you and Principal Gorse out onto the football field. I knew something strange was going on when he led you in here. What's going on?"

I shook my head. Sharelle Bunyan. Our hero?

"It's filling up with water!" Frank shouted. "This is some kind of old holding tank. He left us in here to drown!"

I leaned against the door. "Sharelle, can you call the cops for us? Listen. This is very important. You have to talk to Chief Gomez. Okay? Nobody but Chief Gomez. Tell him that we're trapped in here. Tell him it's urgent—this container is filling with water!"

"Okay," Sharelle replied, "but I'm going to have to go back to the school to get service. This whole field is a dead zone, and I don't want anybody to see me."

"Fair enough," I replied, "but tell them to hurry. And you hurry back. Please!"

The water was up to our knees now. Once the water level rose, it wouldn't take long to push all the air out of the room. We didn't have a lot of time.

"Okay!" Sharelle ran off.

I looked at Frank. He looked like he didn't know what to do. "Let me try standing on your shoulders," he said.

I moved closer and bent down so he could try to climb up. It was hard to see in the faint light, and with the water level rising higher and higher. Soon it was up to our waists.

Frank climbed up my back and tried to steady himself as he carefully placed his feet on my shoulders. With him holding on to my head, I tried to straighten up slowly, and then Frank started to move from a crouch to a standing position.

He was close enough to the hatch to make a swipe at the hose.

I watched, breathless, as his hand pushed at the hose, but it just swung back and forth. It was wedged beneath the heavy hatch door.

"Darn it!" Frank shouted as his right foot slipped. I tried to grab my brother, but he tumbled into the water, where he splashed around, trying to find his balance.

"It's wedged in there anyway," he said when he stood up, holding his head. "I don't think I can push the hose out."

I checked my phone again, which I'd moved to my shirt pocket to keep it dry. "Nothing," I said with a sigh. "I can't take this. There has to be something we can do!"

Frank's eyes kept going back to the door. "Do you hear anything?" I asked. I had to admit, I was wondering how much we could trust Sharelle. Even if she had really run out to call the police, it was entirely possible that it would just take them too long to get here. The water might have filled up the container by then. And Frank and I . . .

I couldn't think about it.

Just as I was losing hope, I heard Sharelle's yell.

"They're coming! I called!"

I sloshed over to the door. "Did you talk to Gomez?"

There was a pause. "He wasn't available," Sharelle said finally. "Or at least that's what they said. I talked to the officer who came to the house the other night. Olsen?"

"Olaf," Frank corrected her with a groan.

Officer Olaf was not exactly the cop I'd choose to hold my fate in his hands. He, well, hated us. And he'd tried so hard to convince us that the Red Arrow was an urban legend. Was he connected somehow?

There was nothing to do now but wait. The water was at our chests now.

No sign of the police.

"Sharelle," Frank shouted, "can you go out front to look for the police and bring them right to this container? I don't want them to waste any time."

"Of course," Sharelle said. "Are you—are you guys okay in there?"

I looked at Frank. I had the unsettling sense that he was sending Sharelle away because, if worse came to worst, he didn't want her to have to listen to us drown while she was stuck on the other side of the door, helpless.

"We're just ducky," I replied, but it was hard to force levity into my voice. "Quack, quack."

I could feel her hesitation. "Okay," she said after a moment. "I'll be right back with the cops. Don't worry!"

I looked at Frank.

"Help me get on your shoulders again," he said simply. "We might as well try."

I crouched down under the water, holding my breath—not really easy with a broken nose. Frank grabbed my shoulders and tried to scramble up. We were both shaking, though, scared and amped up on adrenaline, and this time he didn't even get both feet onto my shoulders before he pitched forward into the water, taking me with him. As he fell, I accidentally inhaled, and water flooded my nose and mouth. I was disoriented and scrambled around with my hands, finally finding the floor and standing up.

"I didn't like that," I said, sputtering.

"Let's try again," Frank said, not looking me in the eye.

We tried again. This time he got up onto my shoulders and took another swipe at the hose before losing his balance. The hose stayed put.

The water was nearly up to my neck.

"Frank," I said.

He wouldn't look at me. "Again," he said. "We have to keep trying."

"Frank," I said again, feeling my throat burn, "what if the Red Arrow's bested us?"

That's when I heard it. Sharelle's voice.

"They're here!" she yelled through the door. "Frank! Joe! Are you okay?"

The next few minutes were a blur. Finally grasping the dire situation we were in, Officer Olaf used his pistol to shoot out the padlock. A few seconds later, the door was yanked open, sending a flood of water cascading onto the grass.

Immediately the water level sank from where it hovered beneath our chins.

We were saved!

. . .

"I suppose I owe you two an apology," Officer Olaf said later that afternoon, as Frank and I sat, still wrapped in blankets, across from his desk at the police station.

Chief Gomez really was out that day, it turned out. His three-year-old daughter had the stomach flu, and he was staying home with her, since his wife had to be out of town on business.

Now Officer Olaf stared down at some paperwork he was shuffling across his desk, as if to avoid looking Frank or me in the eye.

"You do?" Frank asked, raising an eyebrow at me.

Olaf sighed. "It's possible," he said, "that I may have taken your accusations about the Red Arrow less seriously because of my personal . . . well . . ."

"Animosity?" Frank supplied.

"Burning hatred?" I suggested.

Olaf rolled his eyes. "Deeply held suspicion," he said finally, "of you two. But it seems that everything you've told us about Principal Gorse is true. After we got him at the school, we have been interrogating him for a few hours, and he's confessed to being the mastermind behind Bunyan's attack, the blackmailing of Pettigrew Macken, and the explosion at Paul Fumusa's yet-to-be-named restaurant." He paused and looked down at his notes. "He had his connections set up hi-tech surveillance and carry out the actual attacks, since he couldn't."

"See, that's the one I don't get," Frank said, shrugging

and leaning back in his chair. "Why Paul Fumusa?"

Officer Olaf looked at him. "Because he wouldn't pay a 'protection fee' to the Red Arrow to avoid these types of attacks," he said, and sighed. "Which is apparently a form of extortion that the Red Arrow has been pulling in Bayport for years."

I leaned forward. "Has Gorse always been the Red Arrow?"

Officer Olaf signed a paper and frowned. "Well, we still aren't positive the Red Arrow actually exists."

"You said he confessed to everything," I pointed out.

"Correction. He confessed to everything *he* did," Olaf clarified. "He won't talk about the Red Arrow. At all."

Just then we heard the door to the interrogation room open, and two police officers led Principal Gorse out in handcuffs. He had a strange expression on his face that I can only describe as disturbed. He was staring at his clasped hands like they held the secrets to the universe, and I was just waiting for him to rub his hands together and cackle, Mr. Burns–style.

Olaf startled and looked at us. I got the distinct sense that Principal Gorse was not meant to see us there.

He looked up and caught sight of Frank and me, still damp, but very much alive. His eyes bugged, and he pointed one bony finger at us (dragging the other hand with it because, you know, handcuffs). "You!" he shouted, in that low, gravelly voice from before.

The cops leading him tried to hustle him along, but

Gorse dug in his heels. "You think you've stopped it," he said, "but the Red Arrow cannot be stopped. Cut off its head, and another will grow in its place. It's only a matter of time, boys. I wasn't the first, and I won't be the last!"

The cops had succeeded in dragging him down the hall by then. But Gorse twisted his neck to fire one last parting shot.

"Good luck sleeping tonight," he said, his voice a snake-like whisper. Then the cops dragged him around the corner to the lockup, and he was gone.

I looked at Frank. Seriously, had the whole kindly principal thing been an act?

"Yeesh." Sometimes there are no other words.

Frank nodded. He looked at Olaf. "Do you believe us about the Red Arrow now?"

Olaf was still focused on his paperwork. He took out an actual rubber stamp and brought it down on the top of a form. The corner of his mouth quirked up as he replied, not lifting his eyes, "I suppose anything's possible in this town."

RETIRED 19

FRANK

"YOU WANT TO OPEN WITH A JOKE," JOE suggested, leaning back in his chair and taking a sip of his Maximum Mocha. We were at the Meet Locker, trying to get some studying done. "It disarms the audience. Puts them on your side."

"As opposed to whose side?" I asked, my pencil hovering over my notebook. *What do flies wear on their feet?* I wrote, just beneath the title of my newly assigned speech. Answer: Shoos.

Joe leaned over and read what I'd jotted down. "I'd keep thinking."

Right. Well, luckily, I had a whole two weeks left to work on this one. Ms. Jones had forgiven me for going off on a tangent during my last speech. She understood that I was trying to vanquish a longtime Bayport menace. She hadn't completely let me off the hook, though. I'd been assigned a new speech.

Topic: Justice.

Joe suddenly grabbed his phone from where it sat on the table. "Ooh, ooh, ooh," he said, staring into the screen. "I just got service! Look, I have a voice mail."

"Some people ignore their phones while they're studying," I pointed out.

"Some people weren't on the receiving end of a wink from that cute Daisy Rodriguez in algebra this morning," Joe fired back, going into his voice mail. "Why yes, Daisy, I would be willing to explain parabolas in a closer setting. Oh."

Joe wrinkled his nose and replayed the message on speakerphone. We were the only two people in the Locker's back room.

"Hi, Joe. Listen, this is Megan Willensky. You know—Spanish class? Anyway, I'm calling because I have a problem that I think, um, you and your brother could help me with." She paused and dropped her voice to a whisper. "I heard what you did for Sharelle Bunyan?" Her voice rose back to a normal level. "Anyway, call me back. We can meet and I'll, um, tell you all about it. Thanks."

Joe looked at me unhappily. Principal Gorse was in jail, awaiting trial. It took some convincing, but Seth, Neal, and Pett had all gone on record with their stories. Olaf came through with some forensic evidence that tied Gorse to the explosion.

That was all good news, of course. The bad news was that Frank and I had been called into Chief Gomez's office with our dad to go over the Deal again in excruciating detail. We were being watched now, he told us. No more shenanigans. And absolutely no more investigating.

We were well and truly retired.

I looked at Joe sadly, then glanced at the time on his phone. "We'd better go," I said. "Aunt Trudy's making eggplant curry tonight. And you know she's still mad at us for lying to her about my ankle."

Joe nodded and wordlessly put his phone in his pocket. I picked up my notebook, and as I was putting it into my backpack, a tiny piece of paper fluttered out and landed on the table.

It landed faceup, staring back at us like an accusation.

The Red Arrow.

I looked at Joe. Neither of us said anything for a minute. Was this real? Or was somebody messing with us?

"Who?" he asked.

I shook my head. "Could be anybody," I said. "I had this notebook at school all day. Every class."

His brows furrowed. "It has to be a stupid joke. Right?"

I didn't say anything. I grabbed the paper and tossed it in a nearby trash can. I wanted to make a statement, in case anybody was watching.

Frank and Joe Hardy were not controlled by the Red Arrow.

"Let's go," I said to Joe.

Together, we hoisted our book bags onto our backs and sauntered out through the main room and into the sunny air.

Joe pulled his phone out of his pocket and kept playing with it the whole way to the car. Clicking it on, clicking it off. Checking for more messages. Fiddling with the volume.

When we climbed into the car and shut our doors, I put the key in the ignition and turned to him.

"You going to call her back?"

Joe looked at me, hopeful. "Should we?"

I nodded.

There was no use denying it. Sleuthing was in our blood.

Joe grinned and dialed the phone. He waited a few seconds for an answer, then said, "Hey, Megan, it's Joe Hardy returning your call. I heard you have a problem that my brother and I might be able to help you with?"

READ ON FOR A SNEAK PEEK OF THE NEXT MYSTERY IN THE HARDY BOYS ADVENTURES:

MYSTERY OF THE PHANTOM HEIST

FRANK

"Y OU'VE GOT TO SEE THIS, FRANK!" JOE said. "You too, Chet. It's totally sick."

Help, I thought as my brother held up his prized possession, a tablet, for the gazillionth time. Not another lame clip on YouTube!

It was the last thing I wanted to look at as we sat inside the swanky Peyton mansion. I wanted to check out the two slick cabin cruisers docked outside the bay window!

"Will you give us a break already, Joe?" I told him. "I think we've seen enough skateboarding squirrels and break-dancing babies to last a lifetime."

Our friend Chet Morton cracked a smile. "Yeah, but those rapping sock puppets you showed us before were pretty sick," he admitted. "Got any more of those?"

Joe shook his head. "Check it out—it's serious stuff," he said, practically shoving the tablet in our faces.

"You, serious?" I joked. "Since when?"

Joe knew what I meant. Our ages were only one year apart, but our personalities—worlds apart. Joe was always high-strung, fast-talking, and unpredictable. Me—I'm more the strong, silent type. At least that's what I like to think.

"Will you look at the clip already?" Joe urged. "I can't keep it on pause forever." He hadn't put down that fancy new tablet since he got it for his birthday. I couldn't really blame him. We couldn't have smartphones until we were in college, so the tablet was the next best thing. It surfed the Web, got e-mails— even took pictures and videos. Speaking of videos . . .

"Okay," I sighed. "But if I see one squirrel or sock puppet— it's over."

Chet and I leaned forward to watch the clip. There were no skateboarding squirrels or sock puppets—just a clerk at a fast-food take-out window, handing a paper bag to a customer. The clerk looked about sixteen or seventeen. The person behind the wheel had his back to the camera, which was probably being held by someone in the passenger seat.

"Bor-ing!" Chet sighed.

"Wait, here it comes," Joe said. He turned up the volume just as the clerk said, "Six dollars and seventy cents, please."

The driver reached out to pay. But then he yanked the lid off his jumbo cup and hurled what looked like a slushie all over the kid at the take-out window!

"Keep the change!" the driver cackled before zooming off. I could hear another voice snickering—probably the creep filming the whole thing.

I stared at the screen. "Definitely not cool," I said.

"And a perfectly good waste of a jumbo slushie," Chet joked.

"Not funny, Chet," Joe said with a frown.

"How did you find that clip, Joe?" I asked.

"Lonny, a guy in my math class, forwarded it to me," Joe explained. "Lonny was the poor clerk who got slushied."

"Did they ever find the guys who did it?" Chet asked.

Joe shook his head and said, "The burger place called the cops, but so far the slushie slinger's still on the loose."

"You mean it's a—cold case?" Chet joked. "Cold . . . slushie—get it?"

"That's about as funny as those skateboarding squirrels, Morton," I complained. "What we just saw was someone's idea of a dumb prank."

"Yeah, but whose?" Joe asked.

This time Chet heaved a big sigh. "Time out, you guys!" he said. "You promised your dad you were going to slow down the detective work, at least for now."

"Slow down?" Joe asked. "From something we've been doing since we were seven and eight? Not a chance, bud."

Of course, what Joe didn't mention was that we were one wrong move away from reform school. No one knew about the Deal except our family, the police, and our former principal— who had his own issues to deal with now!

"Yeah, but a promise is a promise," I said. "So put that thing away already, Joe."

"Before somebody comes in and sees it," Chet added.

"What would be so bad about that?" Joe asked.

"Because," Chet said, smiling, "surfing clips on YouTube isn't the thing to be doing in the parlor of one of the über-richest homes in Bayport."

Glancing around the posh room we were sitting in, I knew Chet got the über-rich part right.

"Check out the pool table, you guys," I said.

"As soon as I finish checking out those little beauties," Chet said, nodding toward a nearby table. On it was a silver platter filled with fancy frosted pastries.

"Don't even think of taking one," Joe said, pointing to a portrait hanging on the wall. "Not while he's watching us."

I studied the portrait in the heavy wooden frame. The subject was a middle-aged guy in a blue blazer and beige pants. His hair was dark, with streaks of gray, and he was holding a golf club. I figured he was Sanford T. Peyton, the owner of the house, the boats, and the pastries.

I didn't know much about him, just that when the multi-billionaire dude wasn't living large in Bayport with his wife and daughter, he was opening hotels all over the country and maybe the world. The guy was crazy rich. And right now, crazy late!

"We've been waiting in this room almost half an hour," I said as I glanced at the antique clock standing against the wall. "Can someone please remind me why we're here?"

"Gladly!" Chet said. He stood up with a smug smile. "My friends, we are about to be interviewed by Sanford T. Peyton for the honor of working the hottest party of the decade—at least here in Bayport."

With that, Chet turned to another portrait hanging on the opposite wall. This one showed a teenage girl with light brown hair, wearing a white sundress and holding a Cavalier King Charles spaniel with huge eyes.

"His daughter Lindsay's Sweet Sixteen!" Chet declared, pointing to the portrait with a flourish.

"Cute," Joe said with a grin. "And I don't mean the dog."

Chet and Joe were definitely psyched about this party. Too bad I couldn't say the same for myself.

"You guys, we weren't good enough to be invited to Lindsay's Sweet Sixteen," I said. "So why should we work it?"

"Two words, my friend, two words," Chet said with a smile. "Food and—"

"Girls!" Joe blurted out.

"Got it!" I said with a smirk.

The only thing I knew about Lindsay was that she didn't go to Bayport High with Chet, Joe, and me. Which was no surprise.

"Most of the kids at this party will be from Bay Academy," I said, referring to the posh private school in Bayport. "And you know what they're like. Total snobs—"

Chet cleared his throat loudly as the door swung open. Joe and I jumped up from our chairs as Sanford T. Peyton marched in, followed by his daughter, Lindsay. Walking briskly behind Lindsay was another girl of about the same age. She had long black hair, and her dark eyes were cast downward at her own tablet she was holding. As she glanced up, she threw me a quick smile. I caught myself smiling back.

Hmm, I thought, still smiling. *Maybe this job isn't such a bad idea.*

"Have a seat, boys," Sanford said as he sat behind his desk, facing us. Lindsay and the other girl stood behind Sanford, looking over his shoulders at us.

As we sat back down, I could see Sanford studying the applications we'd filled out.

"I see you all go to Bayport High," he said gruffly.

"Yes, sir," I said. "Chet and I are seniors, and my brother Joe is—"

"Daddy, they're cute, but not gladiator material," Lindsay cut in.

The three of us stared at Lindsay.

"Say what?" Joe said under his breath.

"Gladiators?" Chet said. "I thought you needed waiters. You know, to pass around the pigs in blankets."

"There will be no pigs in blankets at this party, boys," Sanford said.

"What kind of a party has no pigs in blankets?" Chet asked.

"Daddy." Lindsay sighed as she checked out her manicure. "Just explain."

Sanford folded his hands on the desk.

"You see, boys," he said, "the theme of Lindsay's Sweet Sixteen is No Place Like Rome. Four strong young men dressed as gladiators accompany Lindsay into the hall as she makes her grand entrance."

"You mean Empress Lindsay," Lindsay emphasized. "And the gladiators will be carrying me on a throne designed just for the occasion."

Joe, Chet, and I stared at Lindsay as she flipped her hair over her shoulder. Was she serious?

"Got it, I think," Joe said. "But you'll still need waiters, right?"

"For sure," Lindsay replied. She turned to the girl with the tablet and said, "Sierra, make sure you get the music I want for my grand entrance."

"'Hotter Than Vesuvius,'" Sierra said, tapping on her tablet. "Got it."

So her name was Sierra. Nice name for a nice-looking girl. I watched Sierra busily taking notes until Sanford's voice interrupted my thoughts.

"If we do hire you as waiters," Sanford said, "there'll be a dress code."

"That's no problem, sir," I said. "Joe and I own suits."

"Oh, not suits," Sanford said. "Togas."

"Togas?" I repeated.

"You mean those sheets the guys in ancient Rome used to wrap themselves up in?" Chet asked, wide-eyed.

I glanced sideways at Joe, who didn't look too thrilled either. Was this Sweet Sixteen really worth it? But when I turned to look at Sierra, I got my answer. You bet!

"I'm sure we can get togas," I said.

"Or some white tablecloths from our mom," Joe added.

Lindsay tapped her chin as she studied us one at a time. She pointed to me, then to Joe.

"Those two can be waiters," Lindsay said.

"Just me and Frank?" Joe asked, surprised. "What about Chet?"

Sanford didn't even look at Chet as he went on with the party details.

"The Sweet Sixteen will be held this Sunday night, being that the next day is a holiday," Sanford said. "That gives us a whole day on Saturday to prepare food, the decorations—"

"My outfits!" Lindsay cut in.

I could see Chet making a time-out sign with his hands. "Excuse me," he said. "But what about me? Aren't I going to work this party too?"

"Maybe," Lindsay said. She turned to Sierra. "Put that one on the B-list. We can always call him if we get desperate."

"B-list?" Chet muttered.

Sanford looked at Joe and me and said, "Well? Don't you want your job instructions?"

I glanced over at Chet, who looked like he'd just been kicked in the stomach.

"No, thank you, sir," I said, standing up. "It's either all of us or none of us."

Joe stared at me before jumping up from his seat too. "Yeah," he said. "Come on, Chet, let's go."

"Are you guys crazy?" Lindsay cried as the three of us headed for the door. "Do you realize how amazing this party will be? You never know who you might meet!"

"If the kids are anything like you," Joe mumbled, "that's what we're afraid of."

I wasn't sure whether Sierra or the Peytons had heard Joe, and I didn't want to find out. All I wanted to do was get out of that house ASAP!

"B-list," Chet kept repeating once we were outside. "Why do you think Lindsay put me on the B-list?"

"*B* for 'bodacious,' dude," Joe said, laughing. "That's you!"

Chet cracked a smile.

"Forget about Princess Lindsay, Chet," I said. "I heard Bay Academy kids can be snooty—but that one takes the cake."

"Wrong!" Chet declared. He pulled a squished iced pastry from his jacket pocket. "I took the cake—on our way out!"

"Oh, snap!" Joe laughed.

As we walked to my car, I had no trouble forgetting about Lindsay, but Sierra kept popping into my head. Then, as if Joe had read my mind . . .

"I saw you watching that Sierra, Frank," he said with a grin.

"You never miss a beat, do you?" I smirked.

Joe shrugged and said, "Just saying!"

Leaving the sprawling Peyton mansion behind us, we walked down the flagstone path toward the private parking lot. I could see my car in the distance right where I'd parked it. But before we could get to my secondhand fuel-efficient sedan, we had to pass a parking lot full of luxury SUVs and sports cars.

"Boats and cars," I sighed. "How many fancy toys can one family have?"

"Not enough if you're a Peyton," Chet said. "Which ride do you think is Empress Lindsay's?"

Joe pointed to a red sports convertible whose vanity plate read LUV2SHOP. "I'll take a wild guess and say that one!" he chuckled.

Chet whistled through his teeth as we went to check out the shiny car. The top was down, so we got a good look.

"Black leather seating," I observed as the three of us walked slowly around the car. "MP3 output . . ."

"Yeah, and I'll bet that's a heated steering wheel," Chet added.

"That's not all it has, you guys," Joe called.

Glancing up, I saw my brother staring at the car door. He didn't look impressed. Just dead serious.

"What's up?" I asked.

Without saying a word, Joe pointed to the door. I turned to see what he was pointing at. That's when my jaw practically hit the ground—because scratched across the gleaming red door were the angry words:

RICH WITCH!

New mystery.
New suspense.
New danger.

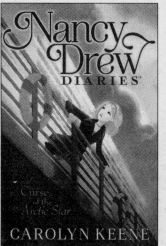

All-new Nancy Drew series!

BY CAROLYN KEENE

The truth is always closer than you think. . . .

"Fast paced, full of great humor, adventure, and surprises."
—JAMES DASHNER, *New York Times* bestselling author
of *The Maze Runner* and the 13th Reality series

"A frighteningly familiar world with an unsettling twist."
—MARGARET PETERSON HADDIX, *New York Times*
bestselling author of the Shadow Children series

MATT IS ABOUT TO BE PUSHED TO . . .